I0647868

the power and the glory

the power and the glory
... for ever and ever

A Philip Vega Novel

by

JANETTE ANDERSON

BearManor Media
2014

the power and the glory
© 2014 Janette Anderson
Janette Anderson Entertainment
WGA West 1732082

All rights reserved.

For information, address:

BearManor Media
P. O. Box 71426
Albany, GA 31708

bearmanormedia.com

Typesetting and layout by John Teehan

Front cover design by Lori Marr

Published in the USA by BearManor Fiction

ISBN—1-59393-399-1
978-1-59393-399-9

Dedicated to Tom Selleck

Chapter 1

"Squeeze tighter, baby, you can do it. And don't squint your eyes like that. How are you going to see what you are aiming at? It's not going to bite you! I might, but the gun isn't," and fifty-year-old Philip Vega slid his arms round his wife's very slim waist. "Squeeze… you've done this how many times before?"

"I have but never with your hands all over my body. You are distracting me, Philip. How can I concentrate with you kissing my neck and your hands everywhere…" and she laughed playfully, enjoying ever minute of her husband's attention. "And shouldn't we be getting ready for Patrick's birthday party? Not every day he turns thirty. I remember last year when I turned that wonderful age…"

Vega interrupted her. "I remember better than you do! You were almost drunk. But then again you had just given me another child," and he nuzzled into her even closer, his head bent right onto her neck letting his long dark hair, that sported a hint of salt, hang onto her face. "Speaking of which, I think we should try again, right now…"

"Philip, I've given you four children! You have Patrick and the twins… twins! They turn sixteen this year." She never mentioned his oldest daughter, Jillie… no one did. And more especially not Donna. "Why would you want anymore?" She knew that was a stupid question. "I mean we have sex five or six times a day, how do you know I'm not pregnant already?" and Emma Vega blushed, something that her husband loved her to do.

"You know something I don't?" he questioned her. "Do you?" just touching the end of her breasts with his fingers.

"Not yet..." She put the gun down on the table. It was only a practice. No bullets involved. "But I might next week. I want to be sure before you go yelling it from the rooftops," and she turned in her husbands arms and leaned up kissing his waiting lips.

"Then if you are not sure, we need to try right now, baby," and his hand slid into her jeans and he left her no choice in the matter as he slipped them down from her body. "No underwear again, Emma... you knew what I would want, didn't you?" and Vega laughed. He knew very well that his wife was expecting this. "So this top unbuttons from the front, right?"

"Philip, we'll be late... Philip..." She didn't offer any resistance to her husband. Emma was more than happy to oblige him whenever he wanted to make love. In fact she couldn't get enough of Philip Vega and him of her as he moved her backwards onto the leather couch that sat in corner of the room.

She glanced at the light dimming in the private gym windows where they had been practicing with the .357. It was getting dark very fast. Philip seemed not to notice.

"Philip, er, it's dark outside..." and she turned slightly in his arms, aware she was totally naked and so was he.

"Really, so... don't worry. We will be there on time. I have better things to do right now," and he laughed at his own joke. "Emma, how would you like to move to Colorado to live?" He was dead serious.

"Really? For good?" Her eyes lit up at the prospect.

"Maybe. I am thinking of letting Patrick run the Vega dynasty. You and I and the kids should think about relaxing..."

She leaned on her arm and looked into his face highlighted by the half light. "You are serious, aren't you? What prompted that? Not what I just said about maybe being pregnant was it?"

"No, baby," he said, as he played with the strands of hair that hung down from his wife's head. "Been thinking about it for a while now. We are all getting older and maybe it's time. If you agree, I will announce it tonight at the dinner. After all, there is nothing else I can give him. It's time, Emma. Time you and I had a life together without me either blowing people away or making deals. I just want you, Em, and the children…" Philip had obviously thought this through. "The Denver house is being renovated right now. Another couple of months and it will look great. Be nice to be there for the winter, and if you are not pregnant right now, I'll make damn sure you are by then!" Vega was dead serious.

Emma went to laugh and realized it wouldn't be the best time to. Philip was not joking. He really did want to retire and be with her. Sometimes she forgot he was twenty years older than her. He had seven children, eight if you counted Jillie and nine if you counted Donna. And still he wanted more. Was it to prove something to the world? She didn't think so. He just wanted more children with her and she was more than happy to give them to him.

While she was thinking, Philip turned her on her back and made love to her one more time. Every time she thought it couldn't get any better and every time it did. He looked into her eyes, questioning her.

"You agree?" he whispered, almost holding his breath.

"If that's what you want, Philip. I do, too… I would love to have you around more, Philip. I miss you when you are gone…" and her voice trailed off. "I love you so much."

"I know you do, baby, and I love you more than you will ever know! So tonight Patrick gets the best present he ever had in his life, even better than the black Ferrari he so desperately wanted. He gets to be the next Don."

Philip swung his legs round and sat on the side of the sofa, pulling his jeans on as he did. "Race you to the shower…" and there was an obvious delighted spring in Vega's step.

Chapter 2

Vega sat on the end of the giant four-poster bed he shared with his wife. He watched her dress, taking in everything he loved about her. He himself was ready to go and as he sat there he slid on his gold Rolex and then stood up. His black, extremely tight-fitting dinner suit moved with him and the Armani shoes he wore complemented the suit. A black silk shirt with a high collar added a final touch, and his long hair hung just onto the collar. As always his .357 was tucked neatly away in the back of his pants, and his cell was attached to the belt on his waistband.

"Emma, I have a gift for you. It is something I was saving for later but I would like you to wear it tonight," and Philip slid his hand into his pocket and pulled out a small box. Opening it, he removed a ring and as he looked at Emma through the dresser mirror where she was seated, he watched her face. She still wasn't used to this, even after all these years, accepting such lavish gifts from him.

Emma half turned to him, her face aglow. Her green eyes highlighted with pleasant dark black mascara and a pretty shade of pink lipstick glossed her lips. Her face was flushed and Vega knew, like he always did, that she was once again pregnant. No one had to tell him. The bright sparkling ring was perfect timing for her. Her long hair was pulled up tightly up onto her head and held with black combs that matched her very exotic and sexy dress… one Philip had picked out for her.

"Philip, I can't take that… it must have cost a fortune." Even she was staggered at the opulence of this gift.

"Emmy, you never had a proper engagement ring, only the wedding band. Now you have one!" and he took hold of her hand and slid the ring on next to her very expensive gold and diamond wedding ring. A perfect fit. He admired his handwork.

"What can I say? It's wonderful. Thank you." Emma threw her arms round him.

He could smell her perfume and it lingered in his nostrils. "You can thank me later, baby," and he had a hard time letting her go. Right at that moment the bedside phone rang. "Thank God for phones," and Philip laughed, moved towards it, put it on speaker and answered it. "Yeah, Mac."

"Everything is ready, Sir. Cars are out front. The family is set to go…"

"All of them?" Philip adjusted his pants.

"Yes, Sir. You and Emma and the children in the limo, except for the baby. Emma said Pip should stay home, also little Andrea and Emma's twins…"

"That's correct, Mac. Not a place to take youngsters. We'll be right down. Patrick driving his own car?"

"Yes, Sir. Has a date with him…"

"Really. About time. I expect they are going on to a club after dinner. I know I would if I didn't have a beautiful wife here waiting for me…"

"Sir…" interrupted Mac.

"You go, Philip…" and Emma pursed her lips at him and mocked his voice. "I am sure I can find someone to bring me home…" she joked.

"Dressed like that, baby, I think any of my sons would be glad to…" he paused. "Sorry, Mac. Forgot you were there. You'll see what I mean in a few minutes."

"I am sure I will, Mr. Vega. I'll get them all into the entrance hall," and with that Mac was gone off the line.

"Ready, baby? Let's get this show on the road," and Philip took hold of her hand, led her out of the suite and across the upstairs hallway.

Emma clutched her purse and her high heels were more than high tonight. She clung to Philip's hand and together they took the stairway down to the hall.

Philip could see the look on Mac's face. And then he looked at his oldest son and he knew that Patrick was still in love with Emma. He glanced sideward at her. He couldn't blame his son. Emma was a sight to behold tonight, any night, but tonight even more so. He figured Patrick would see it, too. He'd been around Emma enough. Philip looked at his son's date. Why didn't it surprise him she would look something like Emma?

Philip's eyes fixed back on Mac, who was certainly appreciating what he saw on Emma. Philip had to admit she did do the black strappy dress justice. It hung from her breasts but was tight at the waist and all the way down. Short, and with a black lace overlay, it was one of the sexiest dresses Philip had ever bought for her, and with her hair up and the long dangling earrings she was captivating. And Philip figured she knew it, too.

He happened to look at his oldest twins. Daniel was dark like him and Orry was the blonde… and Daniel was just like Patrick in looks and his ways. Another son he would have to keep an eye on round his step-mother. It was obvious he more than admired Emma, who didn't even notice any of them in that sense. Orry was much shier and more reserved where as Daniel came right forward and complimented his step-mother.

"You look terrific, Emma." Daniel raised his dark eyebrows and smiled with the old familiar Vega charm, his deep brown eyes fixed on her, and clad in a dinner suit like his older brother.

"Thank you. Your father picked this one out for me," and it was then she turned her hand in Philip's and the brand new ring flashed in the light.

Daniel was the first to see it. "My God, Dad, you gave Emma that today?"

"I did. It's an engagement ring. A little late, but it's for a good reason." Philip smiled. He knew the reason. It wasn't really an engagement ring; it was a thank-you-for-giving-me-all-the-children ring.

Patrick stepped in. "It's beautiful, Emma. It really is," and he paused. "May I see it?"

"Of course," and Emma removed her hand from her husband's.

Patrick very gently held her hand and looked at the ring. He instinctively knew why his father had bought it for her. "Congratulations, Sir," and Patrick addressed his comments to the Don, and dipped his head just slightly to his father.

"Thank you, Son. You can give my wife her hand back now," and Vega laughed and slapped his more than favorite son on the back.

"Yes, Sir. Sorry, Sir," and Patrick looked a little embarrassed.

"You will receive your gift at dinner though and not before. And who is the young lady with you?" Vega cast an experienced eye over the girl standing nervously in the hallway and noted again that she did indeed look like Emma, except she lacked any kind of confidence that his wife had. He also noticed she was very close to Patrick's age. Unusual for Patrick.

Patrick ushered the girl forward. "Elaine, this is my father, Philip Vega, better known in our world as Don Andrea. Sir, this is Elaine Caroni. She is related by birth to Don Caroni and knows all about our lifestyle. I have known her about two months, but wanted you to meet her... and what better day than on my birthday."

The poor girl looked like she was about to faint, but she did know what to do and bowed her head as Philip put his hand out... and she kissed his ring. She looked at the man they called Don Andrea and was in awe. Patrick had forgotten to mention what an imposing figure his father was, majestic and in complete control of the family and any given situation that arose.

"Elaine, the pleasure is ours. I hope you will have a great time this evening, and now we should be on our way. Our reservations are for eight, and it's nearly that now." His words immediately spurred both Mac and Alex into action. Anthony and several other bodyguards were on immediate attention to Vega and the family was swiftly escorted to the waiting cars.

The limo stood ready and Philip, Emma, and the two boys climbed in along with Mac and Alex, the doors still open letting in cool night air.

Patrick called to his father as he kicked the tire on his car and yelled. "My Ferrari has a flat tire, Dad! Damn, do Ferraris get flat tires?"

Philip leaned out of the car. "Take mine, Patrick. You always wanted to drive VI. Now is your chance. Mac, give him my keys."

And PVI stayed in the driveway of the Vega mansion that night and that was the start of their change of life.

Chapter 3

Emma leaned back on Philip's arm that rested on the soft luxurious leather and listened to the chatter in the car. It was happy and boisterous and typical guy talk. Sometimes she missed a female to talk to and that's why she was glad she had produced two little girls. At least she could dote on them whenever she wanted to.

It was only a short drive to the luxurious restaurant that Philip called-home-from-home and the owner himself was waiting at the door along with several valets.

Mac was at the side door just as the car stopped outside Giovanni's... Alex was at the other door, Emma's side. Philip Vega stepped out first and stood there waiting for his wife. Alex helped her out and walked her round to Philip. Daniel and Orry followed her.

"Don Andrea... it is my pleasure to have you at our restaurant once more." He glanced at the lady, her arm on her husband's arm. "Mrs. Vega. You are as devastating as ever... and your sons, Sir..." and it was then that the Ferrari's engines could be heard through the roar of the evening traffic.

Patrick pulled up behind the limo with a screeching halt.

"He drives like you, boss," muttered Mac, who was also dressed for dinner in a rather expensive looking suit, his blonde hair almost longer than Vega's. He and his boss had become closer in the last few years, since they became the proud grandparents of baby Andrea through Vega's daughter, Donna, and Mac's son Marc. A baby that was raised with Vega's other children in the nursery.

"Yeah, he does. No wonder his car has a flat! Make damn sure mine doesn't!"

"Right, boss," and Mac strode off in Patrick's direction in the hopes of sparing the main Vega car… one that was his boss's pride and joy and read V1 for a reason.

"Your other guests are inside, Don Andrea," and Giovanni escorted the party through the big glass doors and took them personally to the table where Vega's guests sipped glasses of vintage wine.

As the party neared the table, Charlie Hill stood up, pushed back his chair and stepped out to great his friend. He smiled the same kind of smile he always had for Vega and for Emma, and put his hand out to Philip, who shook it with great strength.

"Emma, I declare you get younger by the day and definitely more beautiful, if that's possible. Philip you are indeed a very lucky man," and Hill let go of Vega's hand and leaned forward to kiss Emma on both checks. He glanced at Philip first who nodded his approval, and Charlie followed through. No wonder Vega looked so good married to this woman. Who wouldn't?

"Thank you, Charlie. You don't look so bad yourself," and her look passed by him to his table companion. She had a feeling she had seen her before, dyed hair, beads and all. The cut of her dress left little to the imagination and as Emma watched, the lady looked straight at her husband and winked at him. Obviously they had met before.

"Mr. *Black*. Nice to see you again. Been a few years since we met. And this must be your wife. I can see now why you risked your life…" and she stopped short of saying anything else.

"Jonas… Charlie didn't tell me it was you he was bringing. But I am very pleased to see you," and he pulled Emma into the conversation. "Emma, this is the lady that made me blonde and blue-eyed. She helped us all greatly. Without her help, well…" and the whole thing flashed before his eyes and Philip remembered his daughter, Donna and his best friend and bodyguard Pauli. He missed them both immensely.

Emma could see the look on her husband's face and slipped her arm round his waist. Just for a second he was lost in his own world, one she tried hard to keep up with, but he was lost in there all the same.

His mind raced back to Donna, lying in his arms on the beach, the life going out of her and she never knowing that she was his daughter and Pauli, someone he grew up with, shared women with, tawdry nights in low-life clubs with and raced down PCH with, first on Harley's and then in Ferraris. How he wished Pauli was with them tonight to see Philip's son turn thirty. But he wasn't; neither was his eldest daughter, Donna.

"What a waste…" murmured Philip.

"You say something, baby?" asked his wife. She very rarely called him that, especially not in public, and she rubbed his back just slightly and felt the gun in its usual place in the back of his pants.

"Just thinking," and Vega smiled the smile he reserved just for her, and he leaned slightly towards her and kissed her gently on the lips.

"Yep, my friend, and as I said once before, you truly do love her… and you really proved you are great in the sack…" and Charlie Hill smiled and slapped his friend on the back.

Emma blushed, knowing Charlie was referring to her and Philip.

"Charlie, do you always embarrass your friends like that?" asked Jonas as she came round the table to shake hands with Emma. "You have an amazing husband there, Mrs. Vega, and a very loyal one. Yes, ma'am, you really do. You are one very lucky lady," and Jonas put her hand out to Emma and Emma reciprocated the complete gesture that the older lady was making.

"Thank you. I both owe and love my husband very much. He is my world. Without him I could not have gone on…" and Emma stopped, aware that she was caught up in the same moment as Philip.

Philip put his arm round her and pulled her close to him. He could never lose her.

Giovanni discreetly interrupted them.

"Don Andrea, yours and Mrs. Vega's seats?" and the owner and his top waiter stood behind the chairs.

Emma and Philip sat down, Philip at the head of the table and Emma to his right. His twin sons now came to shake Charlie Hill's hand. He was more like an uncle to them as was Mac. They had never looked on them as folks who 'worked' for their father. They took their seats next to Emma, Daniel first alongside of her. Philip frowned but let it go. Vega could remember when Daniel and Orry clamored to sit on Emma's knee, now Daniel would be happy if she sat on his! That thought made him smile.

Jonas was seated on his left and Charlie next to her, and Mac and Alex, invited guests, even though on duty, sat next to them as they waited for Patrick and his date. Everything was set as Patrick entered and loud cheers and happy birthdays rang out seemingly from more than just round the table.

Patrick seemed a little shaken at the lavish array in the restaurant and was ushered to his seat again by Giovanni. He took the seat straight opposite his father right at the end of the table, with Elaine next to him. Patrick was now really surprised as normally this would have been Emma's seat for such occasions and he wondered just what his father had in mind. It could not be the obvious. His father was obviously fit and healthy, despite the scar down his face, and plainly obvious to him that Emma was pregnant again. He wondered if the other family members had noticed, but he had heard that the Denver house was being renovated. Maybe… couldn't be, but hadn't his father been younger when he got the dynasty? Patrick wasn't sure he wanted it right now… He stared at his father whose face was totally unreadable. Emma was a different story. She was glowing and happy and eyed her husband with a kind of lust for living. Was his father ever going to stop having kids? It made Patrick smile. The woman he loved the most was genuinely happy and his father was indeed the luckiest man in the room.

Chapter 4

Wine flowed as did the scotch. Food came and went to the table like there was no tomorrow. Steak, salads, fresh-baked crusty bread, spaghetti, salmon, caviar… anything anyone wanted was served for this event, beautifully cooked and served and the aromas filled the air. Vega drank mainly scotch and Emma water. Another sign. Cuban cigars completed the picture and Philip tried very hard to keep the wafting smell away from his wife. He knew that she hated the smell when she was pregnant and judging by the look on her face she hated them right now, and she moved slightly to her right leaving herself closer to Daniel.

"That's one of Dad's habits I won't pick up… cigars. He and Patrick must have shares in the damn company. Thank God that neither I nor Orry smoke. You okay, Emma?"

"Yes. Your father will never give up the habit," but the smell, even after Philip finished the cigar, was too much for her. "Excuse me," and she stood up from her chair, grabbed her purse and dashed towards the ladies room with Alex fast in tow without even being told to.

"God damn, I put the thing out… now I feel bad. Shit!"

Patrick smiled. At least now they were all sure.

"I'll go after her," and Jonas also left the table.

Charlie leaned across the table. "I guess congratulations are in order, my friend. You sure know how to steel someone's thunder!"

Philip looked at Patrick. "I think he already knew. Where Emma is concerned, he always knows. Remember when I asked him to marry her if anything ever happened to me?" And Vega leaned back in his chair.

Charlie nodded. "I do… and I think he still would, my friend."

"I think he would, too… girlfriend or not and I don't think that Daniel is far behind him." Philip turned around to look for her. No sign. "Excuse me. I need to go make sure Emma is okay… after all it is my fault, on both counts." And Philip was very serious as he left the table.

Mac went to rise and Philip waved him to stay put. His three sons were all there. There was a driver outside with the car, but no one else in here, and Mac was the only gun.

Philip reached the restroom where Alex stood patiently outside. "Jonas is with her, boss. She was sick… I guess we should congratulate you, Don Andrea."

"Guess you should. Makes my decision even easier tonight." Philip paused. "Anyone else in there?"

"No, boss…"

"Good," and Philip pushed the door open and went into the ladies room. No one tried to stop him.

Jonas looked shocked, while Emma sat on a chair in the corner of the restroom.

"You okay, baby?" He asked his wife, leaning down to her. "I'm sorry. I should not have smoked around you… especially now…"

"Does everyone know?" Emma asked, her very pretty cheeks flushing wildly.

"Think they have a good idea, Mrs. Vega. There's a glow about you. You would have to be blind not to see it, and I don't think it's just from being around Mr. Black…" and Jonas laughed, delighted she was one of the first to know that the Vega family were once again to be proud parents. She could see the looks between Philip and Emma. "I'll be right outside if you need me, not that I think you will…" and Jonas laughed again and disappeared out of the luxurious bathroom and stood outside the door chatting with Alex.

"I'm so happy, baby… really, I am… are you?" Vega asked his wife as he pulled her close and tipped her head up to him with his finger tips.

"Very happy, Philip and will be more so after tonight. You are right it is time for Patrick to take over and for us to be a family, especially now." And Emma smiled at him and they both knew why. She stood up to face him.

"Then let's go back and do this. Baby, I promise not to smoke around you again. It was thoughtless of me. I'm sorry," and he pulled her even closer.

"I think, Philip, we should get out of this luxurious bathroom before someone needs it for the right reason instead of the one I think your body has in mind," and Emma laughed a contagious laugh.

"I think so, too, baby…" Philip was happy, very happy, and he ushered her through the door to where Jonas and Alex stood chatting.

"Thanks for waiting, Jonas. Alex," and Philip led the way back to the table and to expectant faces waiting to find out what was really going on.

Philip held the chair out for his wife. Now the faces knew this was serous business. Philip didn't have to do that and very rarely did, except on special occasions. He sat down in his chair as Alex pulled it out for him and then Alex stayed behind his boss.

"Now we are supposed to have cake, but that can wait for a moment. If you have not guessed by now, I, we believe Emma is quite possibly pregnant again, in fact more than think. We'll know for sure in a few days. That wasn't the news we planned to announce tonight," and Philip reached his hand across the table to his wife. "Emma and I will be moving to Colorado as soon as the house is finished." He looked at Daniel and Orry. "Of course, you guys are very welcome to move with us, or go backwards and forwards until you finish school… we'll discuss that later. *All* the rest of the children will go with us, including little Andrea. Mac, Alex and Anthony will go, too." And now came the punch line. "Patrick, you will remain in Los Angeles. As soon as we confirm that Emma is pregnant, you will become the next Don!"

There was silence. Total silence. Alex looked across to Mac, who raised his eyebrows. Mac was happy. That meant semi-retirement for him and Alex would naturally take over from him in Colorado and protect their boss, retired or not. It was time. Now he could spend a little more time with his and Vega's grandchild and that made him happy.

Philip looked down the table at his son. There was a look of astonishment on his face, and on Daniel's and Orry's faces a little apprehension.

"We get to choose, Dad, really?" asked Orry, blonde hair flopping in his face and a crocked smile peeping out.

"You do," replied his father knowing what the studious Orry would pick.

"Colorado. Denver has a great college," and Orry looked happy as Don Andrea nodded his approval.

"May I decide later?" asked Daniel.

"You may…" and his attentions turned to Patrick. "Son, you looked a little shocked. You must have been expecting this?"

"I was… and I am happy," Patrick replied in a lower tone. "I thought you would go on forever, Sir. No wonder you let me drive V1. It had more implications than I knew. I guess you arranged for my Ferrari to have a flat, too."

That was a strange comment and it made Vega think. Ferrari's didn't get flat tires. Not in the Vega driveway. Philip turned his head to Alex and he leaned down to hear what his boss had to say. He nodded. All Emma heard was Alex ask if Philip was armed. She knew he was.

Suddenly she was afraid. Only herself and probably Mac and Alex knew what her husband intended to do tonight. Didn't they? She suddenly had the feeling that the party was on high alert.

Chapter 5

Philip turned his attention back to his guests. Charlie knew instinctively that something was wrong.

"Everything okay, Andrea?" asked Charlie.

"Fine, fine. Just being cautious. Patrick's car got a flat so he drove mine. Normally he would have ridden with us. But he and Elaine want to go on to a club afterwards."

"Maybe we should all go, Andrea... if Emma feels up to it, of course. I haven't been to one for years. You know the right people and places to go. You could get your twins in somewhere."

Daniel's ears picked up. "Could we, Sir? Could we go? We're almost sixteen... Next month!"

Philip changed direction and looked at Emma. "Baby, how do you feel about it? Would you like to go?"

Emma glanced at Daniel's face. It was positively aglow with expectation.

"We can go for an hour or two. I don't think that would hurt. It might be fun, Philip. I promise not to throw up on anyone," and she laughed while pulling the combs from her hair and it sensually dropped onto her shoulders. Emma had learned to seduce her husband, even in front of his children, and she did it very well. Little could they know that her foot was sliding up the inside of his pant's leg.

"If you don't want to dance with Emma, Sir... may I?" Daniel wasn't in the least bit shy about asking.

Patrick smiled. "Whose birthday is it, Daniel? I get first dance!" and he realized what he had said. "After our father, that is."

"Help yourself, Patrick... if the lady doesn't mind... I guess I am so old I can only manage one dance." Philip smiled, but it was a smile that conveyed a lot. There was something behind it. "But first... cake!" and Philip slid his right hand across the top of Emma's legs and left it there.

And then out it came... a huge cake that was enough for the whole family... and someone was singing and everyone joined in.

Philip watched Patrick. He would be the new Don. Vega wasn't sure he knew how to handle this thing of stepping down. He had Emma. He had the children and another baby on the way. He had money. He had everything. That was the point. He did have everything. And soon he would be giving up the power that he had. Was he really ready for this? He felt Emma's hand on his and he looked up into her eyes. He was ready. He still had his deals on the side. Philip smiled at her and squeezed her leg, just gently, but it had meaning.

Charlie watched his friend. He had a feeling he knew what was going on in his head. Vega was only fifty, almost fifty-one, and he was stepping down and he knew why. It wasn't because he wanted to; it was because of Emma and the children, because he wanted time with them. Mac knew it, too.

And it was time for the check. Vega pulled out his card, the one with no limit, and handed it directly to Giovanni. He added a thousand dollar tip and Giovanni escorted them to the door.

"So are we going to a club, Andrea?" Charlie asked. "I can follow you."

"Sure, why not. Emma and I will take VI. Patrick, you and Elaine ride in the limo with your brothers." Vega turned slightly so Patrick would not hear. "Mac, keep an eye on Patrick."

"Boss, something wrong? You sure you and Emma will be okay in VI? We can't protect you from there, specially the way you drive."

"We'll be fine, Mac... soon you won't even have to worry about me."

"Boss, about that. Are you sure?" Mac's eyes questioned Vega.

"I'm sure... just think... two grandpas rocking in chairs on the porch..."

"Right, boss... like that's ever going to happen. You'll probably have another couple of kids first."

"Don't you ever think about finding a woman, Mac? Someone to share both days… and nights with?"

"I've thought about it a couple of times. Maybe I'll think about it again once we get to Denver… maybe. You were lucky, boss. You found Emma. There aren't many Emma's around, or haven't you noticed?"

"Guess I haven't noticed any women since Emma… and Mac, I'll drive slowly. I just don't want Patrick in that car again tonight. Don't know why…" Vega shuddered

"Whatever you want, Sir…" and with that they were all ushered outside to the waiting cars.

They stood on the curb for Hill's car to be brought round to the front of the restaurant. He'd brought the Ferrari that Vega had purchased for him years ago for 'services rendered'.

"Oh, God! Two of them to keep up with!" exclaimed Alex. "Sometimes I wish I had stayed in England! I've seen the way they both drive."

"Sometimes, Alex, you worry too much. Boss just doesn't want Patrick in his car again tonight." Then Mac thought about it… why?

For a second he thought he saw a flash of light, and then it was gone. He looked hard at the building it seemed to come from, but it wasn't there. And then he was distracted by the roaring engine of Hill's Ferrari.

Philip and Emma were comfortably seated in theirs. Vega answered Hill with his own engine, first purring, then roaring. Philip wanted to race down PCH. There was a gleam in his eye and then he thought of Emma and he cooled his jets.

"Go ahead, Philip. One time isn't going to kill me, even though I am dressed to kill…" and she laughed at her own joke, tossed her hair back and raised the hem of her dress a little showing more leg than she really needed. "You can beat him, Philip!"

It was all the incentive he needed and Vega shot down the street with Hill in tow. They curved onto Pacific Coast Highway one behind the other.

"And he wants to step down, Mac… never going to happen!" murmured Patrick. "In name only maybe, but not in reality. He will always be the top gun; both you and I know it." There was almost re-sentment in Patrick's voice, more than there should have been.

Mac heard it or thought he did. And then he saw the flash again. It was there, just slightly, almost a reflection like in a mirror.

"Patrick, get in the limo!" There was urgency in his voice. "Alex call the boss, tell him to get back here. Tell him anything, but make him turn round and come back here now! Someone doesn't want the Vega dynasty to continue and I'm not sure which one they are after, Patrick or Don Andrea!"

Chapter 6

"Go faster, Philip. You can beat Charlie." Emma held onto the seat. Secretly she was scared to death.

Philip felt his phone vibrate on his belt. "Damn," and he let it go to voice mail. It beeped again. "Who the fuck is calling me right now? The guys wouldn't… they know where to meet us! Emma, slide your hand onto my belt and pull the phone off it. Answer the damn thing!" He was annoyed and it showed.

She did as she was asked… tried to anyway. It wouldn't budge and she was getting in his way of driving.

"Never mind, baby. Let it go to voice mail." He powered the gas so hard that he passed everything on the road. He glanced just slightly at her. "You okay, baby?"

"Fine," she replied, shaking in her shoes. But she wasn't going to let him see that.

"Nearly at the club. We lost Charlie back up the road." He looked at the dial. He was doing a hundred. "Geez, sorry, Emma. I didn't realize I was going quite that fast." He slowed down slightly, shifted gears and dropped slowly, but not slowly enough. He tried the brake. Nothing happened. He tried again, and he knew something was wrong.

"Baby, I don't want you to panic… there's no give in the brakes. Means I have to come down by gears only. Make sure your seat belt is tight and hold on to the seat. I know you can't reach the cell," and he heard her gasp. "It'll be fine, babe… I'll just cut the power down," and Philip tried not to let her know how terrified he was they were not going to make it. Still the car stayed around eighty and now he knew they were in trouble.

As good as he was at driving this car; Philip knew they were in serious trouble. The Ferrari had a car phone.

"Emma, flip that switch, yeah, that one," and he nodded his head towards it as tried to keep his eyes on the road. He blinked hard. What the hell did he think he was doing driving this fast with all this scotch in him and with a pregnant wife? Was he losing his mind? His mind wasn't the concern. His wife was.

She did as she was asked as Philip weaved in and out of the traffic. He was hoping whoever was calling would try the car phone. He was right. It rang and Philip let one hand go from the steering wheel for two seconds to answer it.

"Mac, is that you?"

"Boss, you have to come back here. Boss, are you okay?"

"No, Mac... I can't stop the car! The brakes have been cut... no fluid," and he had said it out loud, more than said it, he yelled into the car phone.

There was an indescribable look of terror on Emma's face. Now she knew the truth.

"Boss, where are you? What's around you?" he could hear the Ferrari's engines.

"We're on PCH almost at the club. Passed Charlie way back. I tried powering down the gears. I've come down to eighty now seventy, but its getting hard to control the car, Mac. And Emma..."

"Can you see any grass, anything you can pull over to on your side? Anything, boss? A hill, a runoff... anything... there should be something you can stop the car on..."

"Mac, I can hear sirens... really not surprised... Mac get here as fast you guys can. I'm right near the club... get Emma out of this, Mac... get her out alive. Is Patrick there, can he hear this?"

"Yes, boss, he can, but the twins can't. I was trying to reach you. Someone was watching the cars outside Giovanni's. The flat wasn't an accident... nor are your breaks. You had a feeling didn't you...?"

"I did..." and the roar of the Ferrari's engines once more filled his ears. He didn't want to die and he certainly didn't want Emma to. "Was it me or was it Patrick they were trying to kill? Which, Mac?" Vega yelled.

In his mirror he could see the police cars not that far behind him. First time in his life he was glad to see police.

"Mac, don't let them open fire on us. Make sure they know the brakes failed."

"Charlie called them, Sir... they know, and they know you as Mr. and Mrs. Vega... Boss, if you are near the club there is a turn off on your right, goes up the hill. I can see it on the limo's GPS. About hundred yards. Take it, boss, take it..."

Philip saw it even in the dark. He could see there were car lights heading down the narrow road, but it was his only chance to stop the car.

"Hold on, Em," and he turned the wheel sending the speeding car up the hill, but not quite in the angle he wanted. He was trying hard not to hit the oncoming car whose horn was blaring loudly at him. The Ferrari hit the bank on the left side of the road, turning it just slightly to its right and tipped Philip onto Emma. He hung there in the seat belt almost on top of her, but at least the car stopped, simply because its wheels were stuck in the grass and dirt, with one of them still spinning.

In seconds there were police everywhere. Philip could hear Charlie's voice yelling at the police to let him through. He could see Emma almost under him, her eyes closed.

"Emma, open your eyes. Baby, come on, Em," and he tried to move her.

"Sir, Mr. Vega... can you hear me? Don't move, Sir. We'll get your wife out."

All Philip could see was blue flashing lights in the dark.

"Andrea, do what they say. I'm here. We'll stay with you. Your sons are on the way. Andrea, can you hear me?" and Charlie was allowed to stick his head in the window to talk to his friend.

"I hear you. Get Emma out first, you hear me? Her eyes are shut..." and Vega was frantic.

"She's okay, Mr. Vega. We have her," and paramedics were cutting through the seatbelt and pulling her very carefully out of the car.

"She's pregnant... my wife's pregnant... please be careful with her..." Philip yelled, and his door opened and his belt was cut away also, and arms were pulling him out of his car. "I'm fine, where's my wife..." and Philip rushed round to the other side of the car.

Jonas stood by Emma who was seated on the ground, a blanket wrapped round her. Charlie went with him.

"Andrea, your gun... they're going to want to check you out." Charlie whispered to Vega.

Philip pulled the gun carefully from his pants and handed it in the dark of the car to Hill.

"Another one under the driver's seat."

"Got that one, anymore?" whispered Charlie, pushing his grey hair from his eyes.

"No... got to get to Emma." To Philip this was all taking place in slow motion. He could see the lights flashing and the police and then he could see Emma. She had blood on her leg, but she was wide awake now and looking round for him.

"Philip," and Emma cried out for him. As he appeared, she tried to stand. Jonas helped her, Emma's high heels lying on the ground, her feet on the dirt.

"You're hurt, Emma." Philip was quick to be at her side.

"It's just a cut on my leg. Nothing to worry about. Don't even have to go to the hospital. They said they could treat it right here. Are you okay, Philip? You were tipped up far worse than I was."

"Fine, baby," and he held her close to him, encircling her in his arms, protecting her and nestling into her hair.

Charlie stood next to him marveling that they were both still alive and not even really hurt. If Philip hadn't been such a good driver...

"It wasn't an accident. Someone cut the brake line, Charlie. I could not have stopped the car. Without Mac's suggestion, Emma and I would have been killed."

"I know, Andrea. Mac told me, that's how I was able to get the police here so fast. You have an enemy and a very hostile one, and someone who wants either you or Patrick very dead. And tonight they almost succeeded."

Chapter 7

Emma looked up into her husband's face. "Is it true, Philip... was someone trying to kill you?"

"Me or Patrick. He would have been driving V1 if I hadn't insisted on taking the car. So maybe Patrick... I just don't know who, baby. But we have to find out..." and as he said it the limo pulled up behind the police cars. Philip noticed there were now four cars there and an ambulance. This would probably make the late night news and the morning newspapers. That wasn't good. Everyone would know, but he could hardly buy off the Malibu Police Department... a couple of them, maybe, but not this many.

At least it wasn't so noisy now. The sirens were off, but the lights kept flashing. He could see Emma clearly. Her face was bruised down the right side.

"Let me see, baby." He raised her face with his fingers. "What did you hit? Side of the car?" and he touched her face very gently.

"I don't remember, Philip. Does it look bad?"

"Not bad, but it's there. We should get it checked, babe... maybe the doc can come to the house..."

Mac was round there in a second and Alex stayed with the family, always on guard. Something was really wrong.

"Mr. Vega, you both alright?" and Mac was really concerned for his boss's safety.

"We're pretty much okay," and he turned and felt a pain in his side. He never flinched, not wanting the police or paramedics to see he was in pain. "Car isn't so lucky. We can't touch it right now. The police will want look at it, I guess." Philip cut his eyes to the cops who were under the car looking for clues. He knew the brakes were cut. Would there be clues? He hoped so. Did he want the cops to find them? No, he didn't. But to get the car from them after he had stuck the Ferrari up a bank would be a little bit difficult.

The cops wanted statements. That was also tricky.

He could hear a voice. "Mr. Vega…" A young looking cop was right in his face and one he didn't know.

Charlie and Mac knew Philip had been drinking, and Mac spoke up.

"Can Mr. Vega take his wife home? Perhaps Detective Crowley can stop by and get his and Mrs. Vega's statement. Would that be okay with you?"

Mac was ultra polite.

"Let me radio in and just check that out, Sir," the young officer maybe not more than twenty-five-years-old asked. The radio crackled and hissed.

Emma started shaking in Philip's arms. He wasn't sure if she was cold or it was fright. She couldn't stop.

He slid his arms from around her and slipped off his jacket, bundling it round her shoulders. "I think my wife needs to at least get into the limo. It's a little nerve wracking for her standing here in her condition, and with all this going on."

The officer was most apologetic and allowed her husband to take her to the limo.

"I need Mr. Vega to come back here, Sir…"

"He'll be right back," added Mac, and just as he said it, officer twenty-five-year-old got clearance for them to go.

"Detective Crowley is on his way to Mr. Vega's house. If you would like to take your party home, he will meet you there. One of you will need to stay here until they discover what happened to the Ferrari."

"No problem. Our driver will stay. I'll take Mr. and Mrs. Vega home. His sons are in the limo also. It was a birthday party, and so if it's okay with you, Officer, I will take them now."

"Go ahead, Sir. The gentleman in the other Ferrari can go also. We just need the car and Detective Crowley is a very good cop. He will tell us all that we need to know." Officer twenty-five-year-old looked at the black Ferrari. "I am really surprised they were not killed... both of them. Mr. Vega must be a very good driver to have kept them both alive." He paused, and looked at Mac. "You're his bodyguard right?"

Mac froze.

"I recognized him from his films. You think, I mean not now, but sometime I could get an autograph?"

Mac sighed. "Of course. You have a card, son?" *'Mac, that wasn't bright to call him son!'*

"Yes, Sir," and he handed it over.

"I'll make sure you get one... made out personally to you," and Mac took the card and put it into his jacket pocket. He walked away towards the limo.

The driver was already out and on his way to the crime scene... that's what it was. A crime scene.

Mac stuck his head in the door of the limo. "Emma okay, boss?"

"Yeah, I think it's the cold rather than shock. Can we go?"

"Yes, boss... Crowley will be at the house. Charlie will come back with us also. Right?"

"Yes. I already asked him to. They should stay the night at the house." Philip glanced at his oldest son. Patrick looked pale in the light. "You okay, son? Would you look after Emma for a moment? I need to talk with Mac and Alex." Philip gently let go of his wife. She didn't want him to go and reached her hand out to him.

"Philip..." and she pulled into the jacket.

"I'll only be a second, baby..." and he stepped out of the limo. "Emma is scared to death." Vega paused. He pulled his cigarettes from his back pocket and Mac was there with a light. The events of the night were reflected in his face. Vega was angry and now he could show it... not in front of his wife. He could in front of his men. "Emma and I were nearly fucking killed tonight! This can't happen again!"

"You sure it was meant for you, boss..." Mac didn't finish.

"Maybe me, but more likely Patrick. The son-of-a-bitch that did this has to be found, dealt with and fast..."

Philip was really angry and when that happened someone paid a price. He stamped the half-smoked cigarette into the ground.

"I can't step down, can I, Mac?" Vega's plans spoiled before they had even begun. "Someone doesn't want me to... or someone wants a dead Don. All I wanted was time with Emma as a family... her and the younger children... just a few years in peace and with grandkids. But I can't, can I? That's not what a Don does, is it?"

Mac kicked at the earth beneath his feet. "No, boss, you can't ever step down... and to be honest with you, I never thought you could."

Chapter 8

Vega looked out into the evening air that wafted up from PCH and the ocean beyond. He could still see flashing lights and could smell the sickly smell from half-burnt tires on the Ferrari. He turned to go back into the limo and the pain in his body hit him again. Instinctively he put his hand on his chest and pulled back against the car's side.

Mac saw it instantly. "Boss, you okay?" He moved closer to him, and put his hand on Vega's shoulder.

"Yeah, fine. Just a pain," he lied, "From the seatbelt pulling tight."

"You sure that's all it is? Doc is coming to the house to see Emma. You should get him to check you out also."

"Right. Did anyone notice aside from you and Alex?"

"No, Sir." Mac glanced at the car.

"Good. Keep it that way. Especially around Emma. I think my ribs cracked when I hung from the seatbelt. Nothing serious, but I need to be seen to be the strong one right now." Vega paused. "Mac...you don't think Patrick is up to this, do you?"

"Straight answer? No. He thinks he is...maybe. I watched his face at dinner. If you take us with you to Colorado, he won't survive, boss...or your empire won't."

"Right. So we stay here, or we ship the whole venture to Denver. Fuck!" and Vega smacked the top of the limo. He wasn't disgusted, just a little hurt, but not angry. And someone else agreed with him. But this someone wanted his son dead. He figured the car incident wasn't for him, but for Patrick.

31

Daniel stuck his head out for the limo. "Dad, everything okay?"

"Fine, son… be right with you in the car. Check on Emma for me." And Philip realized what he had said. Instead of asking Patrick, he asked Daniel, an almost sixteen-year-old son for his help.

Both Alex and Mac could see the look in Vega's eyes. And they both knew what he was thinking. Daniel was more like Philip than anyone else in the family.

"Let's get home. I have a feeling this is going to be a long night and not the one we all had in mind. I, for one, didn't…" and Philip stepped into the car.

Mac drove them after everyone else climbed in the limo. Charlie followed and they set off back to the safety of the Vega estate in a much more sedate style than when Vega had arrived there.

Emma snuggled into her husband's arms, and Elaine could not help but notice the closeness of Patrick's father and his stepmother. They were almost like one. She watched them. Philip Vega only had eyes for his wife… literally… and she glanced sideward at Patrick. There was a look on his face she didn't understand. He was staring at his father's wife. He never looked at her like that. Elaine wasn't sure if she should be jealous of Emma or not. What it did tell her was that Patrick wasn't serous about her, even though they had slept together. He had his arm round her and she was leaning on him, but it wasn't right somehow. Orry sat next to Patrick, and Daniel next to Emma. She could hear Alex talking to Mac in the front, very low and almost secretive. Something was going on she didn't understand. How she wished she was home right now. She didn't fit in with the Vega family. They were a unit unto themselves, but strangely she envied Emma. They were roughly the same age, but with two totally different men. One was so confident in his masculinity and his power… and the other one was trying to follow him… But could not walk in the same shoes.

Elaine was still contemplating the situation as they turned into the Vega estate. It looked even more imposing sitting in the flood-lit grounds. She shivered. There seemed to be security everywhere, much more than when they left there. As they neared the house, she could plainly see a couple of Malibu police cars sitting there. She looked at Philip. There was no expression on his face.

As she watched, Philip leaned right down to Emma and whispered in her ear. She nodded just slightly and squeezed his hand. Vega raised his head.

"Mac, drop us at the backdoor. Let us all out. Have Charlie park his car there, also."

"Yes, Sir," and Mac dialed his cell and told Charlie where to leave his Ferrari.

The car stopped behind the limo. Mac was first out and helped both his boss and Emma out. Mac saw Philip wince again. He also saw Philip slide his arm around his wife as though he was aiding her.

"Doc's in your suite, Sir."

"Good. Emma needs him. Mac, come with us. Alex, stay with Patrick and the boys. Keep a couple of the men with you. Have Charlie join us. Elaine, stay with Patrick," and Mac took off with his charges and they slipped in through the back door to the kitchen and into the main Vega suite.

Emma was barefoot and carried her shoes in her hand. She still had her husband's coat draped around her, with her hair hanging loosely round her shoulders. She was cold and her leg hurt. Blood ran down it, implying it was far worse than they first thought. Philip ushered her straight in to their bedroom where the Doc waited.

Mac stayed in the other room with Charlie and Jonas. Philip needed to be with just Emma and the Doc. Jonas stared at the bedroom door.

"She's a very lucky woman to have such attention from a man like that one!" Jonas smiled remembering her makeup job on him some years ago when Philip went undercover. Her eyes positively glowed as they followed him to the door.

Charlie watched her. They had only been dating seriously for a year now.

"You want to swap partners and take him home with you?" laughed Charlie. "He'd wear you out, babe," and Charlie prided himself on the comment. "Andrea has a reputation with women... a big reputation... and how good he is in bed... until Emma came along... She's the only one that knows that now. Perhaps you should ask her!" Charlie thought about that statement a minute. He was actually jealous. His girlfriend wanted a shot at Vega. Then what woman didn't.

Mac smiled. He knew very well of his boss's prowess with women. It had got them both in and out of scrapes for years, but he was fascinated at the banter between Charlie and Jonas. Charlie really was jealous of his boss. That made him wonder. A bit too obvious.

The cell vibrated on his Mac's belt. He answered. "Yeah, boss?" Mac listened. "Be right with you." Mac turned to Charlie. "Drinks cabinet right over there. Help yourselves. Boss needs me in there. I'll be back. Make yourselves at home," and he glanced at Jonas… "Not too at home," and Mac laughed, looking pointedly at Jonas who was crimson.

Mac didn't even knock. At the door, he just went straight into the bedroom and was shocked at the sight that greeted him. Emma sat on the bed, her leg heavily bandaged. Philip stood while the doc finished with his wife. He looked like a very unhappy man… and one who was about to explode.

"I just got a call, Mac. Unlisted number. The caller wanted to know why Patrick wasn't dead!" Vega paused. "And then they said, and I quote… 'and the next time his father won't be around to take the fall.'"

Chapter 9

"**M**y God, boss… male or female?"

"Male… but that means nothing. Where's Patrick?" Vega was visibly shaken. The threat was still for them both. Philip ushered Mac away from the bed and from his wife and the Doc. "Would rather Emma doesn't know all of this right now. She is very shaken and the cut on her leg is deeper than we thought. Her face is bruised, too. Charlie is still here, right?"

"Yes, Sir. You want him in here?"

"I'll come out. Give Doc more time to check on Emma." Philip rubbed his chest.

"Did he check you out, boss? You think your ribs are cracked?"

"Couple I think. Let's go in the other room. You can check them for me. Wouldn't be the first time you did." Philip ran his hands through his hair turning just slightly to Emma. "Be right back, baby. Just want to talk to Charlie…"

"I'll come and join you as soon as the doctor is finished…" Emma said quietly, as she sat there. It was obvious she was in a little pain, and if not that, then she was still scared, not for herself, but for her family.

"She okay, boss?"

"Not really. Wasn't quite the night she and I had planned…" That made him think of her ring. "Baby, you still have your ring on?"

She held up her finger. "Right here, Philip."

Vega smiled at her. "I'll be back," and he and Mac left the room closing the bedroom door behind them.

Charlie greeted Vega first. "How's Emma, Andrea?"

"Shaken. A nasty gash on her leg and a bruised face." Philip unbuttoned his shirt as he spoke.

Charlie saw his girlfriend's eyes light up. She wasn't supposed to react like that to another man, especially not this man, one who was lethal around women.

Philip slid his shirt off. He could have left it open, but he saw the look Jonas sported. He thought it was funny. He could still attract the women, not that he cared to. To him it was a joke. To Charlie it wasn't. Vega sat down on the cream colored couch. Mac felt Vega's chest. His hands went from one rib to another. He counted two broken ribs and a small crack on another.

"You feel that, boss?" Mac asked, knowing full well he did. It needed strapping but that wasn't going to happen.

"Course I feel it… now! And before you say anything… no, I am not going to get it strapped up. Emma will see it!"

"Lucky woman…" the words escaped before Jonas could stop them. She turned away and pretended to be looking at a painting on the wall.

There was a look on Charlie's face that Mac didn't like. He really was jealous of his friend. Vega wasn't interested in Jonas… he was doing this on purpose to force hands… testing the waters… seeing who was who. Mac knew that. Charlie didn't.

"Boss, you can't have cracked ribs like that and not do anything about it. Emma will understand what you have to do…" and Mac stopped as he heard the bedroom door open.

Philip grabbed his shirt and slipped it on trying to hide what was going on, but he wasn't fast enough.

Emma stopped in her tracks. "Party started without me?" she quipped, looking from one to the other. She glanced at her husband. "You doing stripteases again, Philip?" Emma had no idea why she said it, she just did. "I thought that was my job?" and she sidled over to him and stood behind Philip resting her hands on his shoulder. She leaned right down by his ear and whispered into it.

Philip didn't even blink as she made suggestions in his ear and then she walked round and sat down next to him, crossing her legs at the same time while showing an awful lot of leg. Philip finished pulling his shirt on, left it open and slid his hand across her bare legs making sure he didn't touch the bandages.

"Doc left already?" he asked

"Left by the side door. Did you need him? I can get him back, Philip..." Emma didn't finish.

"No need, baby..."

"No, boss... I can bandage your ribs for you..." Mac said sarcastically.

"Philip... why didn't you say something? Mac, get him back here..." stated Emma, turning to the bodyguard.

"No, Emma. Mac can do it... not what I had in mind for us tonight, baby... remember?"

"Indeed I do, Philip," Emma was playing right along with him and she took his hand in hers playing with the wedding ring on his finger. "Did you tell Charlie about the call?"

"Was just about to..."

"What call, Andrea? When?" and Charlie's mood changed as he interrupted his friend. "You got a call? When?"

"Just, in the bedroom. More of a threat really." At a flip of a switch Philip changed gears. "Need to take it very seriously," and Philip stopped playing and slipped his hand just under the hem on his wife's dress. "Someone wants Patrick dead, Charlie. Said I won't be in the way next time." He was about to continue when the suite door opened.

Detective Crowley entered. Tall, white guy with short cropped blonde hair, dark brown suit and obviously a cop.

"Detective, thank you for coming to my home. As you can see my wife was injured in the accident." Vega stood up and moved forward with his hand stretched out to Crowley. As he moved, his shirt flapped back onto his chest. Vega's old scar was still visible on his chest where he had shot himself years ago, and now bruises from fresh cracked ribs appeared.

Crowley glanced at Vega's chest. The scar wasn't his business. The fresh bruises were. "Mr. Vega, you are also injured," and he shook Philip's outstretched hand. "You see the doctor, also, or just your wife?"

"You knew that I didn't?" He looked sideward to Mac.

"My job to know everything, Sir," and Crowley pulled a stick of gum from his pocket, unwrapped it and put it in his mouth. He glanced at the others in the room. "Got you son's statements…just need yours and your wife's. Maybe your, er, guests." The last line was said loosely.

Philip made the introductions. "This is my wife, Emma," and she nodded to him. Philip continued. "You know Mac, my bodyguard, and this is Charlie Hill and his girlfriend, Jonas. They were the ones that called you guys."

Crowley dipped his head ignoring the others. "Mrs. Vega, my pleasure to meet you. Wish it was under better circumstances. I have known your husband a long time. I knew he was remarried, with more children…I didn't know it was to someone like you," and he smiled.

And Mac raised his eyebrows. That wasn't going to go down well with his boss.

Chapter 10

As much as Vega wanted this cop on his side, it wasn't going to be at the cost of his wife.

"My wife is pregnant, Detective Crowley. While you talk with her, I will be right here." Philip sat down next to Emma.

Emma caught the implication the Detective made. Philip slid his arm round her and she nestled into his shoulder. Philip was setting ground rules right there and then so there was no mistake.

"The only thing I remember, Detective, is being in total fear that I was going to die, but knowing my husband is such a good driver, I just hoped and prayed he would be able to control the car." She felt Philip just very slightly squeeze her shoulder. "My husband can tell you far more than I can," and she looked towards Philip, waiting for him to speak.

"I think we both thought we were going to die. I tried the brakes and there was nothing, no give, nothing. Just dead. I tried coming down the gears. Worked a little, but not enough for me to stop. If it hadn't been for Mac here giving me instructions from the GPS in the limo on where there was a turn off… not sure that my wife and I would be alive." Philip said it out loud. Fact was… he knew they would be dead in some fiery inferno.

"Anything you want to add, Sir…" and Crowley licked the end of his pencil that was making notes in his little notepad.

"Should there be?" Vega cross-examined him.

"Can you think of anyone who would want you dead?" Crowley was blunt and to the point.

Philip shot a look to Mac…like don't bring up the phone call now. Philip knew Crowley was totally aware what the Vega household was.

"Probably a dozen or so!"

"That many! Any ideas to pinpoint it more clearly, Sir?"

"Not a one." Vega looked at Mac. Time for his bodyguard to step in. That's what he was being paid for.

"Detective Crowley. Mr. and Mrs. Vega have been through a lot tonight. Perhaps they should rest and I can help you with anything else?"

Crowley got the hint. "Sure, that's fine." He turned towards Charlie. "Mr. Hill can help also, especially as he called us. Seems you were following Mr. Vega. Going somewhere nice?"

"Going to a club for his eldest son's birthday." Charlie Hill wondered if Crowley was really bought and paid for. He looked at Vega, who could almost read his mind, and he nodded just slightly up and down. He was paid plenty, but he had to be seen to be doing his job.

Crowley also knew that Vega wasn't supposed to be in that car tonight. Before the family arrived home, he had talked to Anthony at the house. He had seen the other Ferrari that sported a flat tire, which was why Patrick had taken his father's car and he also knew they had switched cars after the meal.

"You also have a Ferrari, Mr. Hill, exactly like Mr. Vega."

"I do. Why?"

"Just thought the cars may have been mixed up…"

"That could be, except Mr. Vega's tags say VI and mine is a regular plate…and his son's is PV1," and Charlie stopped. That certainly could have been mistaken and that thought hadn't occurred to him, but it certainly had to Philip.

By now Vega had ushered Emma back to the bedroom. He sat on the end of the bed, his face in his hands. The more he thought about it, the more he knew they had faced death. Something so simple, like a birthday party, had made him really think that it was time to go. And now he knew he couldn't. How was he going to tell Emma?

She watched her husband. Emma hadn't slept with this man and been with him now for over six years without learning his moods.

She could almost tell what he was thinking. She wanted to make it alright with him. She knew he had to stay here, protect his family and dynasty. Secretly she wanted them to move; be just a family… she also knew what she had married into. 'The family', not just any old family. The most prosperous one in Los Angeles, and with it came responsibility. She knew what being Philip Vega's woman meant. She knew it the day Philip shot Steven, her first husband, and she knew it when he ended Damien… his own brother, for her… and when Philip almost killed himself over her and saw Marc, Mac's son into a better place. She knew all this the first time she ever set eyes on him, when Philip had pursued her to England only after one brief encounter in the States. She was Philip Vega's wife… and that meant doing exactly what he wanted her do… without question.

Philip looked up at her as she slid out the dress and into a pure silk negligee and robe. She shook her hair very suggestively and then kneeled down beside him, letting her hands rest on his knees. His shirt hung open and she reached up touching the hair on his chest, running her fingers up to his lips. He kissed them, just gently, and took hold of her hands in his and he looked into her eyes.

"Emmy, I am so sorry. We can't go yet. I wanted us to go and be just us. But we would lose everything if…" and he stopped speaking. He said we on purpose. She was part of the 'we'. What was his was hers.

"I know that, Philip. Whatever you have to do, I am always there with you. You think they will try to kill Patrick again?"

"So you also think it was him they wanted?" asked Philip.

"Yes, I do. Unless they watched us switch cars. That's the only way they would know, right?" Emma had brains, too.

"Mac said he saw a flash of light as the Ferrari took off from the restaurant. Someone was watching. But the brakes would have already been cut by then and to have me out of the way would be a great help to them."

"I didn't think of that, Philip."

"You would be a bonus, Em. Take you out, too. No family head and not even a wife around to cause problems." He paused. Maybe they were the right people in the car. "Emmy, I think that everyone should stay the night. We have the room. And tomorrow have a meeting and see what the next move will be. None of us could say much in front of Crowley, even though he is *our* cop. And some things were better left out of the conversation in the other room. Especially the threat. In the family, we take care of our own threats. No damn police force is needed." And Philip stood up to his full height. Shirt still unbuttoned and now his boots lay on the floor by the bed, all he sported was very tight sweatpants that he had changed into. "Come with me a minute, baby," and he took hold of her hand and led her to the door, glancing at the front of her robe making sure no one could see anything they shouldn't. Philip listened at the door and then he text Mac. The reply came back as he wanted it to. Crowley had gone, and Vega opened the door into the lounge and led his wife in with him.

"Mac, ask Alex and my sons to join us. There is something we should discuss, and Mac tell one of the maids to make up one of the spare rooms for our guests."

Charlie Hill looked a little surprised that they were being 'invited' to stay the night. He noted the 'one of the spare rooms' phrase, so Vega anticipated that he and Jonas would share. Presumptuous but accurate. He also wondered why he wanted them to stay.... obviously his friend knew more than he had let on.

Chapter 11

Philip waited until his three sons were in the room. He sat quietly on the couch, Emma beside him. He leaned back on the soft leather of the cream colored couch pulling his wife with him. For just a second his head flopped backwards and he breathed a heavy sigh, which did not go unnoticed by anyone in the room. His long hair dropped back with him and just for that second he closed his eyes. Emma leaned on him and looked up into his face. She was the only one that knew the anguish behind the look.

No one spoke till the oldest Vega sons came into the room and no one missed the look that Patrick gave Emma. She didn't see. She was too busy watching her husband. But Patrick thought he had never seen Emma look so stunning even with a bruise on her face from the accident.

Jonas's eyes fixed on Vega. She watched his face and her eyes didn't stop there. Jonas was in her forties and her own man was in his sixties. Philip Vega was the perfect man. Jonas looked away mainly because Emma caught her staring at Philip and she didn't look too pleased. The last thing Jonas needed was Emma Vega for an enemy. One word to her husband and Jonas would not have a very good future! And Emma had her husband's ear at all times, that and anything else she wanted on him.

Emma drew her legs up on the couch and favored the bandaged one by resting it gently on cushions.

Philip looked at his sons. Maybe Patrick was watching his wife a little more lately. Maybe it would be better if he was married off possibly to Elaine and permanently away from the estate. It would join the two families together. Tomorrow he would talk to Patrick about it. A marriage of convenience. For now, he needed to talk to all of them. He also wanted news of his Ferrari. When he last saw it, it was stuck on an embankment. He hadn't a clue how much damage there was.

He could smell Emma's perfume. He could also feel his cracked ribs starting to hurt. They did need a bandage or two. Perhaps he should let Mac strap them up. He also wanted Emma... damn this wasn't the night he had planed for them. This was a night to make love and plan for their future. He heaved another sigh... and then remembered where he was. He pulled Emma closer to him, not giving a damn what anyone thought. He knew what he wanted.

"Alex, close the door behind you. This is for family... and Charlie." Vega paused. "There has been a change of plans. Emma and I will not be moving to Colorado... not yet. Maybe later, but not now. I will continue to run the family business." Philip looked straight at Patrick waiting for the explosion. There wasn't one, in fact he looked relieved. But then Philip hadn't released the bombshell yet. He was going to wait till tomorrow... why wait! "We won't move till Emma has had this baby... and until Patrick is married!"

Patrick looked shocked and almost dropped the glass of scotch he had brought with him into the room. Mac raised his eyebrows to his boss and Philip smiled a sly smile back. Mac figured he knew what his boss was doing.

Philip felt Emma tense under his arm. He continued. "Orry, if you want to go to college in Denver next year, that's fine. Daniel, you still get to pick." And Vega looked at his oldest again. "But you, son, you need to get married. A marriage to Elaine would seal the houses of Caroni and Vega and that would make a great dynasty for your future." Philip stopped speaking.

Patrick hesitated. He knew that his father was serious and why. He wanted him away from his wife and he wanted this to happen so eventually his father could leave with Emma... and generally what his father wanted he got.

And Patrick spoke up. "What else is behind it, Sir... not grandchildren? You and Mac have one of those. And that doesn't take marriage. I know you wanted to step down, but somehow I don't think you ever will. It's not your style. And now you want me to marry? Since when?" as Patrick's voice got louder.

Vega stood up, tall and imposing, dark and dangerous. Emma had let go of him and leaned back on the couch. She figured this was more about the phone call than anything, but she also knew when to let go of her husband.

"Patrick… you may be my oldest son, but you will never raise your voice to me again… ever! None of my sons will," and he half glanced at the twins. "Is that understood!? Is it quite clear? Is it?" he added, not so quietly.

Instantly Patrick cooled it. Bad move on his part.

"Yes, Sir… but there is more isn't there?" and he dipped his head slightly in utter respect to his father, as he did the twins.

"There is." Philip clicked his fingers just once and Mac handed him a scotch which he nursed in his hands, and then downed it in one go.

Charlie and Jonas never uttered a sound. Hill knew how Vega could be. He had seen him kill a man right in front of his eyes… twice… and now Jonas saw the real Philip Vega. She suddenly found a new respect for the man.

"Before the Doc left, I received a phone call on my cell. Not many people have my cell number as you all know." Philip took center stage. Even in an open shirt and sweat pants he was a commanding figure.

Emma sat up, smoothed her robe down and paid attention to the room, mostly to her husband.

"I quote … 'they wanted to know why Patrick wasn't dead', and followed it up by… 'the next time his father won't be around to take the fall'. So you see it's a double hit. Mainly I am worried about you, Patrick. It was aimed at you. I got in the way, and so did Emma. And that cannot happen again…" Philip stuck the glass out which implied he wanted more scotch. He got it. He turned to Charlie. "I want to hire you and your associates. Your normal rate. I want this person found and fast, before they can carry out the threat."

"Andrea, I can't take money from you… I will be glad to do it, but not for money. What about Mac and Alex here?" Charlie questioned, not wanting to tread on toes.

"They will have another task… which I will discuss with them tomorrow." Vega changed the subject. "How did it go with Crowley? All good, I hope? He gets paid enough by me."

"All good, boss." Mac replied.

Vega nodded. "Good." He looked at the twins. "You guys need to stay home for a day or two, just till this is under control. I think we should all get some sleep now. Been a long day."

Philip looked at Jonas. Her face was blank like this was all a dream, yet she knew what both he and Hill were. He carried on speaking. "Let's meet at ten in the library. Formal meeting," which meant no women. "Emma, ready, baby? You need some rest." He had noticed she looked tired and still shaken. And he needed to talk to her in private, away from prying ears and eyes of all these people. He stretched his hand down to her and she clasped it and he winked at her. She blushed. The bond between them was indisputable. He stopped. "Patrick, your room is your room. Up to you where Elaine sleeps. Same goes for you, Charlie Hill… ." And Vega laughed… "And Patrick, you can have anyone you like to sleep with you… as long as it's not my wife!" and he left the rather surprised room with Emma in tow.

Vega closed the door behind them, leading Emma to the bed and not being so quiet about making love to her.

Mac and Alex knew what his boss was doing and they glanced at the faces in the room. On Charlie's face was a smirk; Jonas looked kind of crestfallen; the twins were like 'way to go Dad'; and on Patrick's face was the strangest look of all. Instead of being the dutiful son that he was, his face was full of anger and he turned on his heel and left the room. He couldn't deal with the whole situation and now it showed.

Chapter 12

The next morning Philip Vega was all business. He sat in the library holding court, behind him Mac and Alex. Anthony and Mikey to his side. His three sons were invited and so were Charlie and Detective Crowley.

If Crowley hadn't known who Vega was, he would now. An open display of the Family life, in full view, both in and out of the house.

"Any news on my Ferrari?" asked Philip, seeming somewhat irritated at even being in the meeting even though he called it. He turned slightly to Mac and he was there with a scotch… even at ten a.m.

"No, Mr. Vega. The boys stayed there last night with the car. Couldn't just leave it there. I think, though, there was a lot more damage to it than to you and your wife. As soon as they call me, I'll drive out there. Is there a garage that you use, Sir?"

"Mikey has the name of the one we use. In one way I want it back… in another way I don't. Nearly damn well killed Emma and me. Maybe I'll get another one, this time not black. Maybe red… maybe."

Crowley proceeded. "Did you remember anything else about the accident?"

"Not a damn thing. Mac can tell you more than I can about the *accident*." Vega stood up out of his leather chair and moved to the window. He looked outside at his younger children playing by the pool. Little Pip, apple of his eye, running round just like her younger twin brothers, Nico and Dante. She wasn't lady-like at all. She was a tomboy like them. She was almost seven and they were near five. And there was his eighteen-month-old daughter, Alessandra, a gorgeous blonde little girl just learning to walk, holding on to her mother's hands. Emma was leading the child round the garden, her long hair blowing in the morning breeze, her body dressed in tight blue jeans and a bright blue T shirt, feet clad in nothing. That was Emma, hands on mom and once more carrying his child. He tapped on the window and Emma turned seeing him there. She waved and smiled at her husband.

Vega was suddenly very aware of what he almost lost… all this and his older son, too. He needed to remember that his family included three other sons. Philip turned back to them all aware they were waiting for him to say something profound.

"Patrick you need to move back in here for the time being. You need protection just the same as I do. Just till we get this straightened out. Daniel and Orry, as I said last night, you stay home for a day or two." And then came the bombshell again. Vega turned and looked straight at his oldest son. "Patrick, you need to get married. Sort out your feelings for Elaine and do something about it, Son. If it's not to be her then date more. But I need you married… preferably to someone who is connected to a family and a good one at that," and his voice trailed off as he turned away and looked at Crowley.

The whole room knew why Philip wanted his son married, even Crowley knew. Vega turned his attentions to the detective.

"So, Detective, anything we can help you with? I would like to find out who cut the brake line... and quickly. If you can't find out… we will! Someone could have been killed last night. And yes, I know the line was cut. Any fool would know that."

"And you are not a fool, Mr. Vega." Crowley cut his eyes at Vega "You have my number, Sir, and now I will check on your car and have it towed to your garage. I bid you good morning and I will be in touch with you as soon as we have news." The detective paused. "Do I need to put in the report that you were injured, Mr. Vega?"

Philip thought for a moment. "Yes, put it in. Might help. Lead a horse to water so to speak. And speaking of which… I didn't see it on the news last night."

"I kept it off there, Sir. To see what you wanted to do." Crowley dropped the pad and pencil he had been holding into his upper pocket on his jacket.

Vega smiled, not so much smiled, but smirked. Smart cop. "Mac, give Detective Crowley a 'thank you' gift and show him on his way."

Philip waited till Crowley and Mac had left and he sat down again and waited for Patrick to explode. This time he did even in front of Charlie Hill. Philip picked up a Cuban cigar; Alex was immediately there with a light while tensions ran high.

Patrick addressed his father formally. "Don Andrea. I do not love Elaine. She is a very nice young lady and if I did love her I would be honored to make her my wife, but I don't. And I do not wish to be married, nor do I wish to live here." There was a kind of panicky tone in his voice. Today he looked more like Philip than ever. Dark, smoldering looks, hair longer and he, too, sported a dark shadow of a moustache… and clothes very similar to his father. Black jeans and black shirt, probably similar because they bought them together. His eyes locked with his father's and both of them knew why he couldn't marry.

Charlie watched with interest, twirling his dark grey moustache with his fingers. He wondered how his friend would handle this. As a Don and Patrick's father he could bring pressure for a marriage if he wished.

Vega tapped the cigar on the ashtray, then put it to his mouth and inhaled deeply, blowing the smoke rings into the air. He watched them swirl all the time knowing Patrick was waiting. Philip Vega was flexing his muscles because he could. Didn't matter if it was his son. Didn't matter who it was. He was making a point. He, himself, had been married way before then. Patrick was thirty and to be a responsible future Don, needed to get his act in gear and fast. Most Don's took a wife or at least a permanent mistress. Patrick had neither… and it was time.

Vega laid the cigar in the tray. "Patrick, I want to retire and live a life with Emma. I had planned to be in Colorado by Christmas with the rest of the family. Last night proved I cannot do that. I need to stay here and protect you. I need you to take my place and right now you can't. It isn't your fault, Patrick. Don't think that. But it would be better if you were married or at least had a live-in mistress and settled in this house. You have to be able to see that. Even Daniel can see that."

And Daniel could see it. Not sixteen yet, but still he knew what his father meant.

Philip didn't know why he said that. But it's what he was thinking. Both Patrick and Daniel looked like him, but Daniel acted a lot more like him than Patrick did.

"Ask her to move in with you. Take it slow, but ask her. It's obvious she likes you. Anyway, Patrick…work on it." Philip was giving him an order… one he could not ignore.

"Yes, Sir." Patrick started to head for the door and stopped just like Vega knew he would. "May I speak to you in private, Sir?" he asked his father.

"You may," and Vega clicked his fingers and they were alone.

"Dad, you know why I can't marry." His voice was pleading.

"I do." Vega looked at his son… this was man to man.

"Then why are you pushing this? Is it because of last night?"

"Yes. Mostly. Patrick I am twenty years older than you and Emma. I need time with her and the younger members of the family. One day that same family could be yours. And before you go thinking I am sick, I am not…aside from a few cracked ribs that really do need strapping." Vega paused and walked to the window, a dark shadow of impending doom. He shuddered. Something about last night was all wrong. Someone was watching what was going on in their household. "Patrick, you will take a mistress. I don't care who it is, even if it's for show. That's up to you. You sort out the details. But you will do it and they will share your suite here. It's our arrangement. No one else in the family will know. We will all be on our guard. Off hand, I cannot think who would want you dead. Me, yes… and I think I might know who it is."

Chapter 13

When the meeting was completely finished, Philip stepped out of the French windows into the courtyard, this time on his own. Sometimes he was tired of the constant shadows around him and that was another reason he wanted to retire. He could see Emma and the children playing down by the pool. Alex had joined them making sure everyone was safe, and Vega glanced around the grounds. Whole damn place looked like a fortress. There was security everywhere. His kids should not have to grow up like this just because of what he was. As he continued viewing the grounds, he could see rose bushes in abundance. Lilies graced the patio walls, ivy clung to the house all hiding the death and destruction underneath it. A mask for the violent world he lived in. Somehow he could not blame his son. He stood there thinking when a voice interrupted him.

"Father," a lighter, younger voice asked.

Philip turned to see Daniel standing there, his dark eyes full of life and his face full of anticipation. "Daniel, you have finished your studies?"

"I have a break." He paused. "May I speak with you, Sir," asked the second son. He was older than Orry by five minutes only, but in real life ten years ahead.

"Of course. You don't have to ask that, son. Let's go and sit down," and Philip realized his chest was hurting far more than it should be and bandages were in order.

Seated in the slick granite chairs overlooking the estate, Daniel began. "I know that Patrick is next in line and I am only sixteen, well next month I will be, but I would like you to consider me if Patrick doesn't want the job." Daniel stopped speaking. He wasn't joking. He was dead serious.

Philip shifted his gaze from the flowers to his son. Daniel was almost as tall as Philip and just as dark and quite possibly one day would be just as dangerous. He had a feeling that Daniel got around a little, especially with the girls. Mikey had told Vega that his son was acquiring a reputation just like his father had when he was sixteen. Soon it would be legal!

"Daniel, I can't say that this comes as a surprise to me. Orry is the studious one and you are so much more like me." Philip didn't laugh or mock him. He put his hand out to his son.

Daniel clasped his father's hand. The grip was firm and had balance to it.

"I shall keep your offer very much in mind," 'more than you know', thought Philip. Daniel had just given his father an alternative even if it would take another four or five years. "I think that one day Orry will make a great attorney for the family. Of that I have no doubt. But you, you have ways like me. I hear from Mikey that you already have girlfriends. Would this be true?"

"I have had a couple. You never said we could not. And I always take Mikey or someone with me. I never go without a bodyguard or two. Have to take them, Sir. I can't drive yet, not officially anyway." Daniel screwed his face just a little at his father, but the respect was there.

Philip saw his second son in a new light. He really was like him in so many ways. How he wished he was older. Then again… maybe not. He liked Emma, too.

"I guess we should get you a car for our birthday, but you will still have to have a bodyguard for awhile. Goes with being my son." Philip paused and looked out at the grounds and to his wife.

Daniel watched his father. "You love her very much don't you, Sir? I can't say that I blame you. Emma is the kind of woman I would like to share my life with. You are very lucky, Dad. You do know that we all know that's why Patrick will never marry, don't you, and you do know he is totally loyal to you?"

"I didn't know you all knew… since when did you know he was in love with her?"

"Since the Christmas in Colorado… Oh, he tried to play it down, but Orry and I figured it out even as young as we were. I feel sorry for any woman that gets hooked up with him. Patrick is a loner, Dad. He always will be. Maybe that will make a good Don, maybe not."

Vega had never heard his son speak like this. It was like he had been spurred into action by the events of the past two days.

"I should leave you in peace, Dad. I just wanted to tell you that." Daniel stood up and dipped his head just slightly at his father and turned to leave him.

"Daniel, walk with me. Let's talk some more. It's not often we have any real family time. You guys are growing up, college, girls… did I miss something there? Promise me one thing. No drugs and no children out of wedlock." Vega stopped speaking. "I am the worst one to give advice on women, except for Emma, of course. I didn't keep my dick in my pants and am no example to you and Orry. Just don't take after me, okay?"

Daniel laughed. "But you picked the right one in the end, Sir, and that's what counts. Don't worry, as much as I like Emma, I am not going to fall for her. She very obviously loves you and likes older men."

It took a moment for the statement to sink in with Vega. His son had a sense of humor. Pity it had taken all these years to find out. Philip saw Daniel in a different light. He certainly had grown up a lot in the last few years. Philip looked at Daniel and could see the twinkle in his eye.

With his arm on his son's shoulder they walked down to the pool to see the twins and Vega's daughter. Emma was the icing on the cake all dressed up in blue. All she needed was a ribbon, one he could undo whenever he wanted.

They chatted continuously till they reached her, little knowing they were being watched. High powered binoculars were trained on them from up in the Hollywood Hills.

The glasses first pointed at Daniel and then switched to Philip Vega. The person watched him intently. They zoomed in even more to get a better look.

Vega was just as they remembered. Six years had not changed him one bit. It was amazing like he had found eternal youth. They switched back to Daniel, now bordering on being a man and a carbon copy of his father. Pity they could not hear what was being said. Binoculars focused on the mouths. Not even with their talents could the person decipher what was being said. Something caught their eye. Behind them, a few feet back, stood someone else just as tall and dark, but older. Patrick came into view. He sported a very displeased look that his father had his arm round Daniel's shoulder.

The binoculars moved slightly to take in the view of the pool and there was the lady of the house with her four children. The binoculars did a double-take. All those children in six years? Man needed another hobby. As they watched, someone they knew well entered the picture. Mac was carrying another child, one with dark features. Could only be Vega's child by Donna. That couldn't be right. The child would hardly be around Emma. The child sure looked like Donna and Vega. When they finished viewing the goings on, they slithered back into the undergrowth where they had come from, noting that the estate still looked like a fortress. Whenever they hit both Vega and his son, it would need to be away from the house… too much power even for a lone gun.

Chapter 14

Lunch was served on the patio. The female half of the party joined the men. Emma, Jonas and Elaine. Jonas and Elaine were still wearing the same dresses from last night. Only Emma had changed, and now sported a short pretty grey and pink sundress that showed her glowing body. They sat in the patio chairs complete with umbrellas for the sun. Only the children ran around closely monitored by two nannies that looked remarkably like army sergeants and picked out by the Don of the house. He wanted his children brought up right.

Vega lounged back on a poolside couch that could seat five. Instead, it housed him and his wife. Philip had also changed into something not so formal. A tight black T shirt and lightweight black pants that fit like a glove... and both female visitors noticed. Vega sat with one arm on the armrest and the other round his wife. He glanced at her.

"Baby, you look a little tired, but still perfect. How about we have dinner in the suite tonight... just you and me, no kids, no anyone else. Mac will stay outside the room."

"I would like that very much, Philip." Emma snuggled under his arm. She realized her leg ached a little and she winced as she moved it.

"You okay, Em?" Philip asked, concerned for his wife.

"I'm fine. Philip, did you get your ribs taken care of?" she replied, just touching his chest lightly.

"I will, baby. In fact when we finish here, I'll get Mac to do it. More concerned about the Ferrari. It was taken to the garage, but I've not heard anything since. I'll give them a call, too, or Mac can." Vega paused more thinking out loud than anything else. "Talked to Patrick and told him what he needs to do. Also talked to Daniel, who wants my job."

Emma sat up straight. "Daniel?" and she looked shocked. "Really? When did this all happen?"

"This morning. I told Patrick he needs either to take a wife or a mistress, but he needs to do it soon…" and Philip stopped speaking aware he was talking to his wife about matters that were only for men. But Emma seemed to understand. She had become more and more a 'Family' wife the last couple of years and someone that Philip could not only talk to but rely on.

Emma looked across the patio to where Daniel sat. He looked more than any sixteen-year-old to be. She figured that he could pass for twenty any day. Her gaze shifted to Patrick who was chatting light heartedly to Elaine. She hadn't really talked to the girl much, but she seemed nice enough and obviously liked Patrick, but she seemed uneasy at being in the Vega compound. Then again, who didn't? When she first arrived there, she was terrified and if it hadn't been for Philip's love and protection she would have run a mile. But Emma had loved him from the first moment she saw him at the wrap party over seven years ago. She had proved that love by giving him two daughters and two sons, and now she knew she was carrying another child for him. At thirty-one she had lived a life one could only dream of and sometimes had to stand back to realize what she had.

"Penny for them, baby," and Philip pulled her gently to him.

Emma looked up into his face and smiled. "I was just thinking about when I came here with you. I was terrified of this place and everyone in it. The only thing I had was you and your love. I didn't know anyone…" her voice trailed off.

"I didn't realize you were that frightened, Em. I'm sorry. I just knew I had to bring you back from England with me or I would never see you again… and that I could not stand." Philip paused, realizing what she was implying. "And you think that Elaine is not right for Patrick?" he had noted where Emma was looking. He smiled at her and pulled her tighter to him thinking what a dark and barren world it would be without her, he, too, remembering back to when he almost kidnapped her from her first husband… and later shot that same husband to keep her safe. He could hear her speaking.

"I know someone better. Alexandria would make a much nicer companion for Patrick. She never married, Philip, and I think she still loves him. She and I stay in touch … just once in a while, and she would fit in here, too."

Vega knew why he was so drawn to Emma. It wasn't just her body and because she loved him. She had a damn good brain that went with those attributes. The suggestion made a lot of sense. He would talk to Patrick later about it… no, he would let Emma talk to Patrick now. It was her idea and he may just listen to her.

"Baby, why don't you take Patrick down to the pool? Just talk to him a little. He might open up to you more than to me. You don't scare him like I do."

"Me? Really? Are you sure?"

"You, Em. This is one time that Patrick liking you so much might come in handy."

"I don't believe you said that, Philip Vega! But I understand what you mean. I'll give it a try. You should talk to Elaine. Flash the Vega charm at her," and Emma laughed, hiding the fact she didn't really want to do this for a reason Philip didn't know. "Between us we should be able to arrange something. Oh, and Philip, my helping hands come with a price."

"They do?" and Vega cut his eyes at his wife and whispered into her ear.

"Yep… that's the price," and she rose up from her husband's arms and the couch.

Philip watched her walk away and approached Patrick. She had done everything he asked her to do and more ever since the day he'd met her. Philip wasn't so sure he would trust him as Emma had done. But he knew one thing for sure. He would never betray her, and certainly never cheat on her. And there had been several chances presented to him and, each time, he had turned them down simply because his love and respect were so great for his wife. Jonas was right. Emma certainly was a lucky woman.

Emma stood in front of Patrick. She had stopped on her way to pass the time of day with Charlie and casually made her way to her step-son… one who was virtually the same age as she was. She smiled at Elaine and spoke quietly.

"May I borrow Patrick for a few moments?" Emma leaned just slightly towards the pair.

"Of course, Mrs. Vega." *'I am sure he will be only too glad to talk with you,'* thought Elaine.

"Emma. The name is Emma," and she smiled accepting the instant hostility from this young woman. Now she knew she didn't want her in the house. A talk to Patrick would be good as long as she kept her distance.

"I'll be back, Elaine," and Patrick stood tall and looked at Emma, the woman he wanted more than anything else in the world, and he kind of knew why she wanted to speak to him. She was his father's woman.

Emma slipped her arm into his, pretending to be his friend, and together they walked a little way down the path, passed the pool and kept on going. She glanced back just slightly and saw her husband rise up and make his way to where Elaine sat.

"Much as I love your company, Emma, I am sure you are on some mission for my father." Straight to the point, his dark eyes smoldering like Philip's.

Emma had noticed Patrick had changed in the last couple of years. He was more arrogant just like Philip was. "I cannot lie to you. I am. He is concerned about you…"

"I know what he is concerned about. Me taking a wife or a something. I gave him my word I would never touch you or even approach you on the subject…" He realized he had said too much and what he had said was a lie. "I, er…"

"Patrick. I have known the whole time how you felt about me. Actually, I was flattered at the time. But I am totally in love with Philip and you knew that, and all I want for you is to be happy. I know your father asked you to marry Elaine, but if you want my opinion, she is not the right woman for you."

Patrick stopped and turned to look at Emma. "You agree?" He was shocked.

"I do. But I do think that if ever my husband can retire you need a strong woman behind you so that you might rule his kingdom as he has."

"And you have someone in mind, right?" Patrick was a head taller than Emma. Just like Philip was.

"I do. And this young lady still loves you, where as Elaine does not." Very matter-of-fact.

"How do you know these things, Emma?" Patrick was now looking down and into her eyes.

"Because you are so like my husband, and a real Vega woman can tell what a Vega man is thinking. Like now." Emma knew all right, and laughed, knowing she had both men's hearts, but she only wanted one of them… and he wasn't standing next to her.

Chapter 15

By the time they had finished talking Philip had also worked out that Elaine was not right for his son. He was kind of sad about it. Those two families would have made a great alliance. But Emma's idea was also solid. An alliance with the Vegas family. Maybe a trip was in order. Take the jet and fly to Vegas. Meet the Alehandro family again. Let Patrick spend time round Alexandria Alehandro, the youngest daughter of his deceased friend and a family that he personally took out the murderer of that friend. It would be a nice break for all of them. Next couple of days. He would have Mac call the hotel and make reservations. Himself, Emma, Patrick and the older twins… and, of course, a ton of security… leaving another ton at the house for the children. He would propose it to Emma tonight.

Philip lounged back in the poolside chair and watched the whole party. Jonas wasn't right for his friend Charlie. She might have been in the business, but she wasn't on the same level as Hill and would never be. Elaine was now looking round her like she really didn't belong. The twins were in a deep conversation about something. Nothing like each other except in looks, they would back each other to the hilt, both strong young men in build and tall, too. Sons he was very proud of. Everyone of them. For no reason his mind slipped back to Donna, his deceased daughter, who never knew who she was. Philip looked across the patio to where baby Andrea played with his children. Five young kids… even if one was his grandchild, and another on the way. Good job he was rich!

Just for those moments he wanted to hold all his kids in his hands, especially Donna, and tell her he loved her like the others, and how he knew he never could. Vega stood up and immediately Mac was by his side.

"Boss, everything okay?" Mac was worried. There was a look on Vega's face that his bodyguard didn't like.

"Walk inside with me. Don't let anyone follow us and I mean anyone, not even Emma." Vega took off inside the library at a fast pace, a very pensive look on his face.

Mac could see the others watching. Alex started to go after them and Mac waved him back. Mac was still number one.

"Something's wrong, Emma. Dad took off for the library with Mac," Patrick looked closer his eyes squinting in the sun. "Mac waved Alex back."

"I should go to him…"

"I don't think you should right now, Mrs. Vega… I think your husband right now is Don Andrea." His tone had changed to one of control.

Emma knew Patrick was right. There was no place for her in Don Andrea's world, once again only in Philip Vega's bed. This she understood right from the start.

"Then let's go sit with Elaine. She looks lost."

Patrick leaned just slightly towards her and kissed her cheek. "That's why he loves you so…" And he took her hand and led her back to the group.

As they sat down by Elaine, Emma glanced towards the library. The door was tightly shut and the shade drawn to the window. No doubt Philip would tell her later what was going on… maybe.

After lunch drinks arrived on the patio. Emma had wine. One glass wasn't going to hurt and she needed it. What could be so important to keep her husband in there for nearly an hour? She needed the ladies room and now would be a good time to go past the library. There was a bathroom right next to it. Slipping inside the house was easy enough, going past the library was another. There were two soldiers posted by the door. She spoke quietly to them and the answer was no. Turning to go towards her bedroom, she heard the library door open and Mac stepped out.

"Mrs. Vega, your husband would like you to join him… at your leisure."

In other words… after she had used the restroom… which she did in double quick time, and was back at the door. The soldier let her into the library, a place that sometimes she would rather not be as generally it wasn't good news in there.

Emma walked into the room. It seemed darker with the shades drawn. Philip stood up and walked towards her.

"Emma, how would you like to go to Vegas? You, me, Patrick, Daniel and Orry, and before you protest about the kids, Alex and most of the household will stay here. In fact don't protest, baby, because it's all arranged." Philip didn't use his power often over Emma, but today he did. He wanted her away from here for a few days while Alex minded the household and Charlie Hill went on a mission for him. Charlie just didn't know it yet.

Emma stared at him. She tried to think of something to say but words would not come out of her mouth.

"Shocked? It was basically your idea, baby. You mentioned Alexandria Alehandro. Well, that's where they are. They are staying at Wynns. Mac made some calls. So that's where we will be staying. I've given instructions to Maria to pack bags for us. You don't have to do a thing except look pretty for me, which you always do, baby. We leave tomorrow afternoon. Get there in time for dinner."

"Philip… I don't know what to say. Your Ferrari and the accident and…" her voice trailed off as Philip's lips touched hers.

Mac smiled and turned away. Both his boss and his wife could twist each other round their little fingers whenever they wanted to.

"And now that it's all settled, Mac is going to strap my ribs up for me so at least I can fly in comfort, and you should get your leg checked one more time just to make sure that all is well. So, what do you think?" Vega flashed his eyes at Mac.

"Sounds wonderful, Philip. A nice break and Patrick will go along with this?"

"Didn't you talk to him about it?" he queered her.

"I did, but I didn't know he was going to meet her tomorrow. You think he go will do it?"

Philip's voice was hard. "I know he will." End of discussion. Vega turned to Mac. "You got bandages?"

"Yea, boss. Right here," and Mac fished them out of his pocket. "You want to sit in the big chair?"

Vega did as he was asked, but continued talking to his wife. "I've never taken you to Wynns, baby. You will like it. Big, great service, pool to lie by, Jacuzzi in the suite. Anything your heart desires and I mean anything." Philip winked at her. He was offering her anything she wanted, including himself, whenever she wanted him.

Yesterday they were fighting to stay alive in a million dollar Ferrari. Tomorrow they were off to Vegas in the Vega jet... luxurious style.

This was Family life at its best.

Chapter 16

Next day came fast enough, breakfast on the bedroom patio that overlooked the pool side of the house. It was a bright, balmy day in Los Angeles, as the announcer on the giant TV in the master suite gave the temperature for the day.

"Nice day for flying, baby. We should be ready about noon, head down to the airfield. Jet is standing ready. Bags are packed." Philip paused. "Damn, Mac pulled these things tight round me. Can hardly breathe, let alone anything else. I need to shower, too." And without warning Philip yelled for Mac just like he did in the old days before Emma. Whole house heard him. Whole house listened.

Mac was there in a shot, his bedroom being next to the Vega main suite.

Mac burst through the door without knocking first. "Boss... what you need?" Like he couldn't guess.

"I need these off! Want to take a shower... now!" Philip growled like a bear. He was not the best patient in the world. "And they are not going back on... I'll suffer."

"Not in silence," muttered Mac, as he undid the bandages. "Morning, Emma. How's the leg?"

Emma smiled. She knew Mac well. "Fine, just fine. Everyone getting ready?"

"Yes, ma'am. After your husband sent Charlie and Jonas home so late, and Patrick dropped Elaine back at her place, it went quiet. Charlie was moaning about some task you had given him, and Elaine seemed happy to be gone from here. The twins were overly excited and you and Mr. Vega just disappeared."

"That wasn't my fault... Philip wanted to..." and Emma stopped dead and looked at their faces.

Mac was laughing and Philip was trying hard not to.

"You!" and Emma glared at her husband and stormed off into the bathroom.

"Your wife still gets embarrassed, boss, even after all these years. She's a very cute young lady. Still looks like she did the day we kidnapped her from England. Pity she didn't have a sister."

"Was quite some trip, wasn't it, Mac?" murmured Philip.

"It was. Destiny lay in your path. Your future, boss."

"It did and it's been an ongoing adventure with her..." and Philip looked towards the bathroom.

"I'll leave you in peace, boss. Some things you don't need me for... Meet you both downstairs at noon." Mac turned on his heel and left the luxury of the Vega bedroom as Philip entered the bathroom behind his wife.

Noon came fast. Emma had said goodbye to the smaller members of the family, almost a little teary eyed. She knew it was only for a few days, but still she missed her offspring when they were away. She knew she had to go with her husband. That was her job in this family.

The limo waited outside, its engines purring in the noonday sun. Two excited young men waited in the car, and next to it stood Patrick, his eyes smoldering with a dark sense of foreboding that usually was sported only by Philip. Patrick glanced at Emma, radiant as ever in a very sleek short black dress and black high heels to match. Her hair was pulled high on her head and still she looked so much younger than his father. His father, the Don, looking totally powerful and in control and Patrick knew that he meant business. Maybe it wouldn't be so bad seeing Alexandra again. They had, after all, shared some special moments a few years back. Maybe these few days would be good. His expression mellowed.

The trip to the airport produced nothing more than small talk. Emma had covered the bruise on her face very well and the dress length just covered her small bandage she now sported. She was as excited as the twins over going to Wynns and was trying very hard not to let the rest of the car see it.

It wasn't that far to the airport and boarding the plane was even easier. Mac and Mikey ushered them onto the flight. Mikey hadn't been on many trips with the Vega family not in all the years he had worked for them. Now was a nice chance to shine. He was still in his forties, dark like Vega and very determined to rise up in the ranks. Single and a soldier… through and through. A couple more soldiers waited at the jet. Alex was assigned nursery duty for the days they were gone… someone Vega could trust completely with his children… him and four more bodyguards.

Mac filled Mikey in during the flight. Philip drank scotch and Emma chatted to Daniel. Patrick sat with Orry and they passed the short flying time just having big brother talks.

Emma found Daniel very easy to talk with while Philip talked to Mac about security at the hotel. They had booked a suite, a very large suite with three bedrooms and a small suite next door for the security. No expense spared and Philip knew that the hotel also had good security that patrolled the private entrances to the way-above-average suites. Philip also knew that Gabrielle and her two daughters were there. Alexandria was the objective; Mac had discovered that Felicia was also there and recently divorced from her husband. That could spell trouble. They were to visit Don Giovanni and his wife who were taking a small vacation, but Felicia had held a grudge against Philip since he broke off the affair with her years ago and more so that he 'ended' her brother for killing her father. Felicia had never forgiven him on either subject.

Philip stared out of the window, holding the scotch on the rocks in his hand, sipping it once in a while. He was thinking back to the few months that he and Felicia were together. He always had a liking for younger women and she was no exception. Great body, very driven and someone to sleep with… and that was it. He never promised her a future and there certainly was no past. He could have let her down easier rather than just dumping her like a rag doll. But he had never loved her. She was just a playmate, sounded cruel now when he thought about it. Maybe he could have let them all down better. Conscience was catching up lately. Maybe that was because he loved Emma so much and she made him realize what he had been missing before her. All he had before her was one night stands, so to speak. But he did hope he didn't have to see Felicia too much. It was hard not to be mean when she hadn't even cared that her own brother and his friend shot Don Alehandro to death. She hadn't even cried! Alexandria had. Her mother had, but not Felicia. All she cared about was her brother. Vega's hand tightened round the glass and he smacked it down on the armrest so violently that the scotch flew out of the top of the glass.

They all turned to look, especially Mac. He knew when his boss was angry and this was one of those times.

"Something you need, boss? Fresh drink?" and Mac took the glass from Vega's hand.

"Yeah, .357!" Don Andre replied, sincerely meaning it.

That raised some eyebrows.

Emma moved down the plane to him and sat down by her husband. "Okay, baby?" she asked trying to soothe his obvious temper that was about to flare, and she leaned just slightly his way letting him get a great look at her body.

He calmed slightly taking in the view.

"It's Felicia, right?"

Vega looked shocked. "It is. How did you know?"

"Mac told me she would be there. It's in the past, Philip. You can't change it. Don Alehandro is dead and we are going to see Alexandria, not Felicia. She's in your past also… and she was before me, Philip. And I'll be with you. I'll always be by your side, you know that. Till death us do part."

Philip thought that statement was very appropriate. More than Emma could know and he really hoped it didn't come to that.

Chapter 17

As the flight touched down in Las Vegas, Philip wondered what he had done to deserve a woman like Emma. She completely understood him. He didn't find that scary, just consoling that someone did... especially her.

Ten minute ride to the hotel... or it seemed like it. Nice limo picked them up and when you were spending the money the Vega family was you expected the best.

In Vegas, Philip was known to both ends of the spectrum... the film end and the other one. Even the private entrance of the hotel was busy.

Philip Vega did not go unnoticed as he stepped out of the limo with his wife in tow. He was an impressive figure, like an Armani male model, totally clothed in black and expensive shades. If one didn't recognize him as a movie star one would know he was a mob boss. His wealth and power preceded the figure and as his sons stepped out of the limo behind him there was no doubt he was a Family man. He slipped his hand round Emma's smaller hand and he walked with confidence into the lobby, Mac on one side and Mikey on Emma's side.

They walked with ease and a click of heels through the lobby of this magnificent hotel. Marble floors, high ceilings, chandeliers, flowers everywhere one looked, service at the drop of a hat. And security that one could see a mile off. Mac signed them in. Vega waited on purpose. He wanted to see how it was dealt with there at Wynns. Impressive enough.

"All signed in, boss. Let's get you all settled in," and Mac lead the way to the elevator.

The whole party followed with security tight at every turn.

"Nice place. Hasn't change a lot since the last time we were here... right, Mac?"

"No, boss. It hasn't," and Mac looked around him. Amazing what money could buy. Sometimes he envied his boss. But Mac had done well by him and amassed his own little nest egg.

Reaching the elevator was fairly easy. They boarded the glass-sided dome that sped them up to the 16th floor and the private luxurious two-floor suite that awaited them. As they stepped out in the very obvious opulence Emma could only stare around her. Even the twins hadn't been anywhere like this. The three of them walked through the rooms till they got to the far ceiling-to-floor windows of the suite. In front of the twins and Emma was a view to die for. The evening took on shade and a million lights lit up the sky. She was drawn to it like a magnet, her face pressed against the glass.

Philip and Patrick stopped at the doorway watching her every move. Patrick glanced to his left and there was the biggest bed he had ever seen... one which no doubt would get good use.

"You have the suite next door to this one, Patrick. Mikey has a room in that one also. Don't worry they are very private. Mac stays in this suite and so do the twins. We are all taken care of. And now when these guys have finished exploring, we should go to dinner. We are all suitably dressed. Emmy," he called to his wife. "Baby, let's get ready for dinner. There will be plenty of time and opportunity to gaze through that window!" He smiled as he said it, acknowledging the bed was right opposite the window.

Emma blushed and turned to smile back at her husband. "I've never seen anything like this, Philip, not ever."

"You wait till you see the bathroom, Emma," and Daniel yelled to her from the richly appointed room that was loosely called a bathroom. "Come and see," Daniel yelled.

"Son, she might want to use it before we go to dinner." Vega called Mac to him. "Show them their rooms and let's get this show on the road." They were all dismissed.

Emma wandered round the suite trying to take in this opulence.

"Emmy, we'll go over the whole place later on. Let's eat, babe…" Philip was just a tad irritated. He was used to this. Emma wasn't.

"I'm sorry, Philip." And she ran into the bathroom.

"God damn it, Philip. Take it out on your wife, why don't you?" Vega was angry with himself. He stood by the bathroom door. "Baby, I'm sorry. I just want this settled with Patrick. Emma," and he smacked the door frame. "Emma," and he tried the door handle to the bathroom. It wasn't locked. He opened it and Emma was looking into the mirror. Tears streamed down her face. "Baby… I certainly didn't mean to make you cry. It's just…"

"I know what it is, Philip. And I shouldn't be such a baby. Sometimes I get concerned for you. Maybe I should just stay here tonight." Emma murmured.

"You will do no such fucking thing! You are my wife and where I go you go, and it's me that should be apologizing… not you. Let me see your face," and Philip pulled her very gently to him. She wasn't one of his soldiers he could boss about. She was his reason for living. How could he reduce her to tears? He clung to her looking into her face, one that was hurt. "God, Emma. I am sorry. Please don't cry. It will never happen again, baby. I will never make you cry again."

Emma believed him. She knew what the stress was doing to him. It was slowly killing her husband. She saw it today on the plane. It was time for her to be the strong one of the two.

"I'm fine, Philip, really. I know you didn't mean it. I guess I really am pregnant. Getting weepy at the drop of a hat." And she stifled her tears, her back pressing onto the gold plated knobs on the washbasin.

"Would you mind if you were, baby?" He asked her very cautiously.

"Of course not, why? Are you upset if I am?" Emma thought that was a strange question from him.

"Good grief, Emma. I would be delighted. I hope we have six kids. But it's your body that has to go through this, not mine, and I remember the last one you struggled a little more. But no, Em, I am delighted. Why do you think I bought you this ring?" and he held her hand so he could see the ring better.

"To show everyone I am yours…" quipped Emma.

"Smart lady……that's exactly why!" and Philip laughed making light of it but really meaning it. It was why and to thank her all in one go. She really did have brains. He drew slightly back from her. "You know, Emma, since you came into my life there has been no one else. You do know that don't you? And there never will be. No one can part us." Philip didn't give her a chance to answer him, just leaned down and kissed her, holding there, loving every inch of her. He was breathing hard as he rose up from kissing her.

He took her hand and led her back into the bedroom.

"Philip, we don't have time. You wanted to go to dinner…" and her voice trailed off as Philip continued kissing her and he pushed her gently down on the soft white fluffy quilt, tossing the pillows out of his way with his free hand. "Philip…"

"Emma Vega, will you be quiet… they can wait." And Vega shed the clothes he needed to and hers all in one go.

"Don Andrea… is that an order?" she asked looking into his smoldering brown eyes.

"That's an order, Mrs. Vega, and you know you have to do what the Don tells you."

Chapter 18

"Where are they?" Patrick paced up and down in the main lounge of the largest suite. He ran his fingers along the top on the grand piano. Spotless as one would think.

"Patrick, why don't you sit down? I am sure your father will be out momentarily. Probably something came up..." and Mac stopped aware of what he had just said.

Mikey cast him a look as much as to say, 'do you know what you just said'... and he flopped down on a giant cream couch that could have made a bed.

Even Daniel stopped in his tracks at the comment and looked at Mac. Orry didn't even notice and carried on inspecting the downstairs butler's pantry, having never seen anything like this in his young life.

"Good for Dad. If Emma was my wife, I wouldn't hurry down here either." Daniel was straight to the point and he sat himself down by the window and looked out at the lights half wishing he was his father.

Mac could see the change in Daniel. He was more like his father every day. Pity he wasn't older. Daniel would make a good Don. He didn't let emotions get in the way. As on cue, Mac's cell rang.

He grabbed it. "Yeah, boss. Okay. We are all here. See you in ten minutes." And he put the cell back on his waistband. "Your father will be right down, so I suggest, Patrick, you might want to pay him the respect he commands." Mac had said out loud what he was thinking. Maybe not a good idea, but it was the truth.

Patrick walked across the room towards Mac... and changed his mind about saying anything. He knew baby brother was well and truly waiting in the wings and if Patrick was honest Daniel was more like his father than he was. As he was thinking things over, the door into the lounge opened.

"Sorry to keep you all waiting. Emma and I had to sort some things out."

They all noticed she had changed into a very glamorous, extremely short silver and black dress, black stockings and heels. Her hair hung on her shoulders and she looked like she had been crying, but she also looked like she had been handed an inner glow…and that was very obviously put there by the Don.

"Mac, you reserved the table?" Philip looked straight at his bodyguard, his jacket slung over his shoulder showing the change of shirt to one that matched Emma's dress. It was slightly undone at the neck.

"Yes, Sir. And I invited the guests that you asked for, all five of them." He glanced at Emma. "And may I say, Mrs. Vega, you look stunning"

"Indeed you do, Emma," added Daniel. "I was can see why you were both late to dinner."

Emma blushed and dipped her eyes.

"See, Emma, even my sons think you look great! And you want to stay home. Not tonight, my lady. You have a job to do, and where I go, you go, always. So, let's go meet the dinner party." Subject closed and he slid into his jacket.

Vega was first into the private elevator and Emma next. There was hustle and bustle about them as the elevator shot down to the first floor where the doors opened. Mac stepped out first and looked around him. The place was alive with people. Mikey stood on the other side and Philip Vega and his lady stepped into the real world that Wynns had to offer.

Vega was majestic and he stood there surveying the entrance to the restaurant like he owned every inch of it. Philip wore shades as he looked around mainly because he didn't want anyone to see where he was looking. He offered Emma his arm, which she accepted gladly, and together they stepped across the marble-floored lobby to the restaurant. They were shrouded by bodyguards and followed by sons as they all made a spectacular entrance.

Heads turned to look at the obvious wealth of the family entering the restaurant. Some recognized Vega as the movie star, but most knew better, and one or two dipped their heads as he passed by. Waiters stepped out of the way as the party was shown to their table.

The others guests were already seated round the large circular table. Don Giovanni rose to great Philip Vega. He extended his hand in greeting and Philip let go of Emma, clasping the old man's hand, kissing him on both cheeks.

"E cosi bello vederti," proclaimed Vega to his friend.

"E anche voi," replied Giovanni, and a large smile spread itself across his face.

"What did they say?" asked Emma to Daniel.

He translated the greetings. "I can teach you Italian, Emma, enough so you understand our father. But I think you got the gist of what they are saying. He only really speaks like that to another Don. It's in respect."

"I thought it might be," and Emma looked at the two men and then down to Maria, who had a warm smile on her face. Emma leaned down to her, and Maria was quick to put her arms up to the younger woman.

"Mrs. Vega. It's so nice to see you again after all these years. You look so well, my dear. Don Andrea must be treating you well, I hope?"

"He treats me very well," and she saw the look on Maria's face as she caught sight of the diamond ring. And now Emma really knew why he had bought it for her. "Beautiful, isn't it?"

"Emma… you know what a ring like that means?" Maria gasped, her face older and wiser. Her hair neatly tied up in ribbons and her dress matched her grey hair.

Emma smiled. She thought she knew… now she wasn't sure.

"It means you are his for eternity and God help the person who tries to part the two of you. He will kill them. You belong to Don Andrea," and Maria looked straight at Felicia, a young woman she did not care for too much, her friend's daughter or not.

"I wasn't aware it meant that much…" but it did explain a lot. Why he insisted she wore it. Maybe she also should pay him more respect than she had of late. "Thank you for telling me."

"Maria… so good to see you again. It's been too long." Philip jumped into the conversation and greeted his friend's wife very sincerely.

"Don Andre. You look marvelous. Your wife is looking after you very well. And those must be your sons behind you. My… how your twins have grown. I hear you have other twins."

"We do," and Philip slid his arm round Emma for all to see and hear him. "We have twin boys and two little girls," as Philip put his hand on Emma's stomach. "We are expecting another child."

"Then many congratulations are in order. We should order champagne." And the older Don called for the waiter.

Philip laughed. "That's how we got another four children in the first place!"

Mac stood behind the chairs and offered his boss one first, and Mikey pulled the chair out for Emma who sat right next to him. The sons seated themselves and Patrick sat very pointedly next to Alexandria, stating how nice it was to see her again. And it was. He surprised himself. He was actually glad to see her. She had changed little and was still the wide-eyed young woman he had bedded. Maybe there was hope.

Hellos were said all round and Gabrielle greeted Vega warmly considering he had had her son terminated for participating in her husband's death. Felicia was another matter. She glared at Philip, who couldn't help but notice she looked like someone who had seen the bottom of a bottle one time too many. He sincerely hoped he hadn't added to that, but it was long ago and she was not his concern in any way shape or form. What she did was her business, but she had lost any youthful look and had donned the stature of an old maid, her hair going grey already and her dress old fashioned.

Vega removed his shades and dropped them into his pocket lounging back in his plush red velvet chair. He looked at his oldest son chatting to Alexandria. Might happen, might not, but it was a start. Daniel and Orry were talking very politely to Don Giovanni and his wife, and Emma looked a little lost, staring intently at her ring.

Vega rested his arm on his wife's chair, his hand touching her shoulder. He could see the hate in Felicia's eyes for both him and his wife. She was the second one on his list of suspects and was one that had a certain kind of power.

Chapter 19

Emma picked at her steak. More pushed it around the plate.
"If you don't like that, Em, I can order you something else. You have hardly eaten anything for two days, baby." Philip was concerned. She wasn't eating enough for one let alone two.

"Not hungry, Philip." Emma was staring around her. She could see something off in the distance and could hear cheering. She wondered if that was the casino. She could also hear music from the other side of the restaurant and just see people dancing.

"You have to eat, baby. It's not just for you… someone say something to you tonight?" He had a feeling she knew more than he did.

"Not really," and she looked into his face. "Well, kind of. I learned the true meaning of this ring…" and she looked at him very expectantly.

"I wondered if you had. Well, now you know. When a Don gives his wife one of those rings, it's for ever. No going back," and Philip moved the strands of hair from her face and leaned towards her a little more and kissed her lips. She smelled good to him and his lips lingered there. She had become his obsession.

More than one at the table noticed.

"Would you like to dance, Emma?" her husband asked.

She smiled kind of coyly. "I would."

Philip stood up. He turned slightly to Mac, who stood behind his boss. "Going to take Emma to dance. Stay close."

Mac nodded in agreement. This would be a good place to take someone out and he needed to be on his toes.

Mikey pulled Emma's chair out and she stood up smoothing her dress down, but showing how slim she really was. Almost too slim and certainly didn't look pregnant.

Philip took her hand in his and led her away from the others and their stares.

"Like being in a God damn fishbowl," muttered Philip to himself. "Can't even go dancing without them all staring at us," and Philip took Emma towards the dance floor.

On his way there, complete with bodyguard, Philip stopped twice to speak to people he knew. He didn't introduce Emma, but he did keep her close to him. The couple stepped onto the dance floor as others stepped out of their way.

Philip took his wife in his arms and held her tightly to him. She slid her arms round his back and could feel the gun in the back of his pants… even there. He was a head taller than her and she nestled into him moving in time to the beat.

Mac stood at the side of the floor quite obvious who he was with. His eyes scanned the dance floor. His boss was right. He did need an 'Emma'. One night stands were not enough.

One dance turned into two. Emma looked up into Philip's face and she smiled. "You want a boy or a girl?"

"One of each," and Vega laughed and he realized the only time he was really happy was with his wife… and his children, and now he knew that Patrick better make this quick. He stroked her hair and let his fingers linger there and kissed the top of her head.

Finally the music stopped.

"Would you like to try the casino? You ever gambled, Emma?" Philip asked.

"Once… and it was so worth it…" Her smile was rich and full.

"Touché, my lady. Let's go and see if you can win me some money." He turned to Mac. "Get the twins. Leave Patrick with Alexandria and the rest of the security. Bring Mikey."

And it was done

They headed for the casino in grand style and were met at the door by a very official looking man in a dinner suit and bow tie. He sported a goatee and was flanked by two bodyguards. Tall and obviously the man in charge.

"Don Andrea," and the man stepped in front of Vega. "Any table you like, Sir. Would I be thinking no limit was in order?"

"You would, Giorgio. I am surprised you remember me from the last time I was here." Vega had changed since then with his long hair, moustache and slight beard.

"How could we forget you, Sir? You brought us very good business that evening." His gaze took in Emma and the young men with them. "Your wife, Sir... and two of your sons? No doubt they are sixteen this year."

"That would be correct." Vega was to the point and never flinched. "This is my wife, Emma Vega."

"Mrs. Vega, it is our pleasure to meet you. You want anything, you just let us know. Anything at all." Mr. Tux dipped his head to her and Giorgio was politeness itself.

Emma nodded her thanks. For once she was speechless. This was Don Andrea's world she had stepped into and fine and fancy it was.

Giorgio led the party to the dealer's tables. "Did you want a private game, Sir, or just a game?"

"Any game is fine. It's for my wife. She wants to try." Vega smiled. He knew Emma had no clue how to play.

"Not this game, Philip... I would rather try roulette."

"Really, baby?" That caught him off guard. "I didn't know you could play." Vega raised his eyebrows.

"Just a little from watching, er, someone else gamble away my money at roulette and cards..." she stopped. She had never told him that before and perhaps now was not the right time to.

"Would your wife like to try a game or two, Sir?" asked Giorgio, kind of amazed.

"I think she would. Let's see what she can do. A talent I didn't know she had." And Philip ushered his wife through to the tables and found her a seat.

Giorgio made a space big enough round Emma so that her husband and Mac stood with her. Mikey and the twins stayed in the background, watching with a certain anticipation.

Philip gave her an amount of cash which Giorgio turned into chips.

Emma sat on the chair and crossed her legs letting her dress ride up. The whole table of men noticed. They also noticed whose woman she was. Vega stood right behind her with such an air of authority almost daring anyone to look her way. Everyone who knew Vega knew he always carried a gun and so did his bodyguards, and quite possibly more than one each.

Emma was oblivious to the men watching her. Her focus was on the game as the wheel began to spin.

Philip watched in amazement as she doubled her money and then tripled it. The rest of the table was in shock. Her joy was boundless and she clapped her hands in glee, her hair tossing back and forth as she turned to tell her husband.

Philip whispered in her ear. He knew that cameras rolled in the casino walls and no doubt she was now marked. He knew because they did in the ones he owned.

"I think, gentlemen, I have won enough for tonight, and my husband awaits," and Emma slid off the chair and took her husband's hand, looking extremely pleased with herself.

"We will have your money sent to the suite, Mrs. Vega. I hope your stay here is pleasant," and Giorgio smiled at her, a genuine pleasure at being around her. The table was out-smarted by a very beautiful woman with a very dangerous husband and one who knew the rules very well.

Chapter 20

"**M**y God, Emma, where did you learn to play like that?" and Daniel didn't hide his delight, and bypass his father to congratulate his step-mother.

"On that score, I had a good teacher."

Once again Emma was the centre of attention. Even shy Orry joined in the congratulations as the little party headed back to the dining room and to end the evening with drinks.

"Who were they cheering at, Dad? We could hear it from here," commented Patrick.

"My wife… she won several thousand dollars, actually ten thousand," and Philip pulled her chair back for her out of sheer respect, a move that didn't go unnoticed by anyone.

"Emma?" Patrick almost chocked on his wine.

"Do I have another wife?" asked Philip.

"No. Just I am shocked." Patrick was more than shocked. Emma certainly was no pushover. He should keep that in mind.

"So are we all," added Daniel, sitting down next to his step-mother.

Patrick couldn't help noticing that Emma and Daniel were forming a closer bond in the last year or so. If it didn't bother his father why did it bother him? But it did. He leaned back in his chair, his hand just resting on the back of Alexandria's chair, a lady who seemed more than happy for Patrick to be back in her life.

Drinks arrived at the table. The cash arrived at the table and Philip asked for it to be kept in the hotel safe and a receipt brought to him.

The hotel sent them a magnum of champagne for the table. Seems even they were impressed and Vega was understandably proud of his wife. And Emma downed at least two glasses. She was extremely happy and leaned towards her husband, whispering in his ear so that only he heard. Vega nodded his head just slightly in response to her.

"Ladies and gentlemen," Vega stood up, unaided. "My wife and I bid you goodnight. She has a better proposal for me upstairs than you do down here," and Vega wasn't shy about the opportunity that awaited him. "Patrick, I will see you in the morning. I bid everyone goodnight."

Emma stood and wobbled just slightly on her high heels. Her face was aglow with happiness, that and champagne. And Patrick's jealousy was written all over his face.

"Mac…" and the three of them left the table. "You see that, Mac?" asked Vega to his bodyguard.

"I saw it, boss. I was hoping we were wrong," Mac was sincere and followed Vega to the elevator.

"So was I. But seems like we might be right. I just wonder who else is on it. They wrecked a nice Ferrari… my Ferrari and almost killed us. Take us to the suite, lock us in and come back down here. We'll be fine. Have one of the guys stay outside the suite door just in case. Watch out for the twins, especially Daniel. He wants to be me and that person knows that! Bad situation."

Vega wrapped his arms round Emma's shoulders who appeared not to be hearing the conversation between the two men. She was too intent in getting her husband into bed and wasn't shy about it. She snuggled into him making a really big play for him.

"Too much champagne… good job she's already pregnant…" Philip stopped speaking. It was what he needed. "See you in the morning, Mac. Tomorrow night, you get the night off. Find someone for you."

"You need some help there, boss?" asked Mac, almost envious.

"She's fine… just gets a little crazy after that much champagne. Makes my life very interesting, so does the sex…" and Vega stopped and smiled. "No, I don't need help. But thanks."

This was a side of Emma that Mac had never seen.

"You might want to turn the TV up when you come back, Mac."

Mac did a quick sweep of the suite and made sure everything was fine and left his boss there. As soon as the suite door was shut, Vega picked up his wife in his arms and carried her into the bedroom. He kicked the door closed behind him and laid her on the giant bed, pushing pillows out of his way.

"No, Philip," and she tried to stand, peeling her own clothes off as she did, and then turned her attentions to her husband, sliding him out of his suit with great expertise. He never wore underwear and this made her life easier.

As he lay on the bed, Emma kissed him long and hard, and with a gleam in her eye. She didn't stop with his chest and carried on down as he ran his hands through her hair, then leaned back in ecstasy as Emma fulfilled her quest and Philip's satisfaction.

While Emma and Philip made love till dawn, fruit baskets and flowers watched them from the dresser by the big glass windows. The one basket contained a camera of sorts and was maybe in the wrong suite. Certainly it should not have been hiding in a Vega bedroom.

At seven a.m. Philip reached for his cell. His long arm managed to grab it and with one hand expertly text Mac.

The reply came back that Patrick had spent the night with Alexandria.

"Thank God."

"You say something, baby?" asked a very sleepy Emma, her one arm wrapped around her husband's chest, her hair hanging down her naked body.

"No, baby. Sleep some more. It's still early. We will have breakfast in the room here. I'll wake you in a little while. I just want to go in the other room for a minute. I'll be right back."

"K," she murmured, not really hearing him.

Philip slipped out of the bed and pulled on pants. He opened and closed the bedroom door as quietly as he could and met Mac in the lounge.

"So he actually was there or just wasn't here?"

"Guard said he was there all night with her."

"Thank God. Maybe Emma and I can have a life."

"Yeah, boss. Maybe we all can. You and your lady are making us all quiet jealous."

"Could you hear us?" Philip looked shocked and looked down at himself just dressed in pants.

"I could and the twins could. Not sure about the other security."

"Fuck..."

"That, too," laughed Mac, as the suite door opened and Patrick appeared.

Patrick was dressed exactly like the night before and had come to tell his father that he would be seeing a lot more of Alexandria. He was just about to when his father's bedroom door opened and an angel stepped out.

"Philip, where is breakfast? For some reason I am so hungry. Must have been the long night we had," and Emma stood there just with a sheet wrapped around her, hair hanging down and sun from the window at her back. She shook her hair very sensuously.

Just as she entered, the suite door opened and the twins came on through. Jeans and shirts all prepared and ready for the day's sight-seeing in Vegas. Daniel stopped and caught site of Emma. Both he and Patrick, two sons with a single thought.

And now more than one person in the room looked at her like she had dropped from heaven.

Chapter 21

"Doesn't anyone knock around here?" asked Philip very agitated that all three sons came into this part of the suite uninvited. "Patrick, please wait here. You two," and he looked at the twins, "out. Wait downstairs in the lounge. And Emma, go back to bed, baby. I need to talk to my son. Mac will order food for you." He pulled her to him and kissed her lips in full display of his family and then sent her through the bedroom door with a pat on her backside. "Mac, order her breakfast and then come back here."

"Yes, Sir." He was gone after Emma.

Vega sat down and leaned back on the couch. He yawned. Two hours sleep was catching up really fast. He glanced at his watch. "So where did you spend the night?"

Vega was treating his oldest son like he was sixteen again.

"With Alexandria. That's what you told me to do, isn't it? Or is that wrong, too?" Patrick was a very unhappy man. "I'm thirty, Sir... not sixteen."

"Then start acting like that. You know the rules. You either take a wife or a mistress when you become a Don. You always knew that." And Vega slammed his hand down on the arm of the couch. "Or don't you suddenly want the job? You always wanted it. You dreamed of it when you were Daniel's age and now, suddenly, you are backing away from it." Vega stood up and poured himself a scotch. It went down in one go. He poured another one, and it wasn't even eight a.m.

There were only bodyguards outside the room, not that Vega felt threatened, especially as he turned his gun could clearly be seen in the back of his pants. But so could something else. Patrick could not help but notice the marks on his father's back.

Patrick clenched his fist. He couldn't go on like this. He had tried very hard to subdue the feelings he had for his father's wife. But whatever he did they would not go away. He'd moved out of the house and now being the Don would bring him back there.

The bedroom door opened and Mac reappeared. "All ordered, boss. She ordered enough for two or three people," and Mac went to follow it up with something about last night, but thought better of it as he saw Patrick's clenched fist.

"Any problems, Don Andrea?" Mac only called Vega that in times it was needed.

Vega turned and caught sight of his son and the look on his face. He slammed the glass down on the wet bar top.

"Enough of this, Patrick. She is my wife and is your step-mother. Give her and me the respect you should... or you are no son of mine. We came here for your benefit to find you a wife... and for a small vacation and to get away from the house, not to play games."

"Me?" yelled Patrick. "You are the one playing games. You know I can't be around her. It rips me apart and yet still you flaunt the sex life you share with her. Everyone can see it, even the twins. No wonder you had nine, no ten children! How many more are there? What about Felicia? She gave you one you are hiding somewhere?"

Vega raised his hand and went to strike Patrick just as the bedroom door reopened.

"Philip, no! He is your first-born son!" and Emma rushed forward and grabbed Philip's arm. "Mac, stop him."

"Why, Mrs. Vega? Don Andrea is right. His son shows no respect for your husband!"

But Mac did move closer to Vega and Patrick.

Patrick looked at Emma who was now sporting a robe, her body still clearly detectable through the silk.

"Don't try anything, Patrick. Your father has every right as the Don," and Mac had his hand on his gun.

Only because Emma was holding Vega's arm did he not hit his son. She pulled his arm down by his side, something not even a man would attempt. But she had not even been thinking that in the heat of the day Vega might hit her instead. His muscles were apparent in his arm and she had a hard time holding him, but she clung on, figuring that the cracked ribs were slowing him a little. The bruising on his chest was still very plain to see.

Patrick knew his father had meant to hit him and if he was honest he deserved it.

The main door burst open and Daniel came rushing through with Mikey in tow.

His first words were to his father.

"Sir, are you alright? We could hear your voice downstairs…" and Daniel turned his head to his step-mother. "Are you okay, Emma?" He never asked Patrick. "Mac, a problem?"

"No problem, Sir." Mac didn't have any problem calling him that, in fact he was gaining respect for the younger son rather rapidly and losing it for the older one.

"There's nothing happening, Daniel. I am moving in with Alexandria at the winery and we will see how it goes. If all goes to plan," 'my father's plan', he thought. "I will hope to marry her, and then…" and Patrick paused. His very first mistake and he knew it. He also saw both Mac and Daniel come to his father's side.

"And then what, Patrick? Someone is trying to kill us. Or had you forgotten that little fact. My Ferrari is a right-off. A car that you were driving before me the other night, because your car had a flat tire." His eyes were narrow and his face angry.

"And you told me to use it." Patrick argued, defending himself… Just as angry, yelling back at his father.

"I did, not knowing the brake line was cut! What we don't know is when it happened! Was it for you or me?" and Vega backed off his son, more out of frustration than anything. He continued, "Crowley called last night. Brakes were cut right through. The garage was surprised they didn't go earlier. But 'they' didn't know you would be driving it, right? It was supposed to be me even though the person that called mentioned you. But the car is gone, history, and if it wasn't I wouldn't want it back. It nearly killed me and much more importantly Emma, you know 'the love of your life'!"

Emma let go of Philip's arm. She was shocked that father and son would go at each other like this. Hadn't this happened before with Marc? Emma backed off towards the door.

"Stop it, both of you!" and she turned and fled into the bedroom, slamming the door behind her.

"I need to go after her. We will continue this later, but, Patrick, remember, you are not the Don yet!" And Vega disappeared into his bedroom to find his wife.

And now Mac took over. "Patrick, I will be very clear. You don't ever disrespect your father again. Mikey will back me and so will most of the household. Maybe you should not be the next Don. I for one will not work for you. Don Andrea had been working for this empire for ten years when he was your age. He had children, responsibilities and this empire grew rapidly. Nothing stood in his way. And I mean nothing and no one! So now you do what your father asks or you tell him now you want no part of this. Today, Patrick. Today! None of us will stand by and see you ruin him or his empire."

Patrick was stunned. Had his father put Mac up to this? He thought not. This was Mac speaking for the Family and he knew he meant it. If the family didn't back him he was done. He glanced at Daniel who was totally stone-faced and ready and waiting to be trained. Now Patrick had to make a big decision. Either go with what he had been told or get out now. He had no choice but to follow through on his commitment and the decision was made... and there was no going back.

Chapter 22

"Emma, I'm sorry that was in front of you." Vega never apologized like this. It wasn't his style.

Emma turned to face him from staring out of the window and across the dimming early morning lights of Las Vegas. She wanted to run to him and throw her arms around him, make love to him again, be there for him... and she knew that wasn't the right thing to do. If anything ever happened to this man... she would die. And now she felt he was being opposed and, indeed, he was by his own son. She looked at him standing there. He was so macho and a natural born killer. That didn't scare her anymore. It's just what he did. This time he had to make the first move.

Philip could almost read her mind. "Emmy..." and he held his arms out to her.

She ran to him and clasped him to her and he buried his face in her hair. They stood there moments like that sharing the time with each other, one not now complete without the other. Emma was the chink in the Don's armor, and his son knew it. But she was also the chink in his son's and Vega knew it.

"Mac's talking to Patrick. Sit on the bed a minute, Emma. Patrick will take more notice of Mac and that's not good. You would think he was Mac's son..." and Philip stopped speaking as they both sat down on the oversized bed, one that a few hours ago was the focus of pleasure. That brought back a ton of memories for Philip. He dismissed them quickly.

"Philip? May I ask you a question?" She was very timid.

"Of course, baby." He looked very inquiringly into her eyes.

"Were you dreaming of Pauli and Donna last night? Well this morning really."

He was shocked. "How did you know?" he had tried to keep his dream quiet.

"You were talking about Donna, then me, in your sleep."

"I was. I dreamed that Donna and Pauli were running along the beach in the dark. I could hear gunshots. Someone was firing at them. I thought it was Rossi. I could see them running, trying to get away. Pauli took a bullet so that Donna wouldn't. Still they kept running, running, the ocean lapping calmly at their feet. Then the faces changed. It wasn't Rossi firing at Donna…" and Vega stopped speaking. Sweat ran down his body. He was obviously upset.

Emma wished she hadn't mentioned it. But she had to know. "Who was firing, Philip? Who pulled the trigger?"

Philip let go of her and stood up moving to the window as he did. He didn't want her to know the rest.

"I have to go shower, baby. You want to join me? Then we can go do some sight seeing." Philip was tired and it showed. It wasn't the first night he had had the dream. It kept popping up ever since the accident.

"I'll go if you answer me." Now Emma wondered if she had overstepped her bounds, her husband or not. She kept a brave face. She couldn't let him see she was a tiny bit scared of him.

Philip went to say, 'you'll go anyway, baby,' and changed his mind. She was his wife, not his mistress, not someone he ordered to have sex with him, not that he had ever had to do that. He leaned back on the glass window. It was warm on his back and the early morning sun streaked his hair. He dropped his stare and looked at the floor and could see his shadow there, like some angel of death.

He sighed deeply as if all the problems of the world sat on his shoulders. "Patrick. It was Patrick firing the gun. He shot Pauli in the back. I miss Pauli, Em. I miss him and Donna!"

Emma jumped off the bed and ran to him. "Oh, Philip. I know you do. She was your daughter and he was your best friend. How can you not miss them? That was insensitive of me, but I had to know."

And now was not the time to tell her husband that Patrick had made a pass at her a few days before the accident. He was drunk and it was no excuse, but she had the feeling someone else knew. She had watched Mac keeping a close eye on Patrick since then. She knew if she told Philip he would go right out there and choke his son to death. She threw her arms round her husband.

And Philip had not told Emma that Donna's face had changed also and before his nightmare ended it was her that Patrick shot. He could see her falling into the ocean and he was trying to grab her hand as she slipped from his grasp… and Philip lost her.

Vega clung to his wife and then he lifted her up in his arms and walked with her into the shower, totally oblivious that someone was watching them the whole time, and not until the flowers needed changing would anyone know that the camera was there.

Outside in the lounge Patrick was gathering his senses. Mac had just told him that the household would not follow him with this attitude towards his father… regardless. He could see the satisfied look on Daniel's face. Daniel was out to be the Don. Here it was again, the younger son wanting the role instead of the older one, and it was obvious that the soldiers were in full support of the younger. Was Daniel really only almost sixteen? He was almost as big as Patrick was and way more powerful in his thinking. He would run the Family with an ironclad fist, and he wasn't a threat to his father.

Patrick wondered if Emma had told his father. He thought not. He probably would be dead by now. Why in God's name did he make such a pass at her? He was still thinking about it as the bedroom door opened and the pair walked out.

The mood had passed and for now Mac was letting it go with Patrick.

"So, Daniel, where is Orry? You guys wanted to see the town. Let's do it. Patrick, I am sure you are bringing Alexandria. She ready to go?" Vega didn't miss a beat. "Mac, a limo, if you please, big enough for all of us … and a car to follow. Everyone can have a day out. Maybe even dinner out tonight. We'll see about that later." Vega took control just like he always did. Just then his cell vibrated, the one always attached to his belt.

Vega looked down at the number and let it go to voice mail. He would get the call later.

Orry was ready in a flash and the whole group ended up in two limos. Emma was a little relieved that Patrick and Alexandria were in the other one. She had managed it at the house to be kind and helpful to Patrick, but, in this close proximity, it was becoming more difficult.

Daniel sat back in the car watching his father. He could learn so much from this man. The way he handled the bad, but enjoyed the good life. And that's what he wanted to learn. How to get the woman he desired and how to keep her happy, just like his father kept Emma obviously very happy. She was on her fifth child and he figured there would be another couple before they were through having children.

Vega noticed his son watching him. "Penny for them, Daniel."

"I was thinking what it would be like to be you, Sir. You have a beautiful wife, all of us, wealth, power and an empire." Daniel was very determined in his speech.

"I do and it didn't come without a heavy price tag." Philip thought about that statement for a moment. How true was that, and he glanced at Mac, who was listening to the whole conversation. He went for it. "You think you could handle that?"

"I do, Sir," replied Daniel crisp and clearly.

"So do I, Son. So do I," and Philip leaned back on the luxurious black leather of the limo.

So Mac had told Philip at some point what he suspected had happened. Emma didn't know where or when he had, but Philip knew and she was sure than he would confront her about it in his own time.

Chapter 23

Emma turned slightly and looked at her husband. He saw her and whispered in her ear.

"We'll discus it tonight, baby. I know, that's all… and I commend you for not betraying my son." He slid his arm tightly round her shoulders and held her there, a smile for her on his face. "Today we enjoy the day. Tonight we dine." He paused and looked at his bodyguard. "Thanks for the text, Mac."

So that's how Philip knew. Mac had put his thoughts in writing so to speak. Risky, but a way not for them not to talk about it outright. Philip didn't look angry; in fact he had congratulated her. She leaned back on him and as her T shirt slipped from her shoulder, he slid his fingers under her bra strap and left them there. Black suited her. Even the T shirt and jeans were black, but today she wore sneakers for walking later. Philip wore black as well, and the sons followed suit, except Vega wore his usual boots.

The limo turned into the strip and glided through the traffic with an air of 'someone important was coming'.

"Thought we would tour round a little and stop and take in the view from the sidewalk. You know… walking." His voice was sarcastic. He wondered if his kids were up to that these days. It would be good for them.

The limos pulled over near the Bellagio. Emma wanted to watch the fountains cascade in the air to music. Not just any music but Bocelli. That pleased Philip immensely, that she was learning to love the music he did. She jumped out of the limo excited, like a little child, and was talking away to him about the colors of the fountains and the shapes they formed.

Philip followed her, amused at her and her antics. Orry was in hot pursuit of her as she took off to view the fountains with a security person following in close proximity of his boss's wife and son… gun always on his hip. Emma and Orry were way ahead and Philip and Daniel were at a leisurely pace behind them.

The other car stopped and Patrick and Alexandria climbed out. Patrick didn't even look in his father's direction. He knew that Vega knew what he had done and probably by now that the household was against him. The smart thing to do was lay low and move in with Alexandria, marry her and then perhaps his father would be happy with him again. An idea sprang into his head. Marry her in Vegas. He knew she would go for it. She made that abundantly clear last night. They would be there another couple of days. Obviously his father and Emma were having a good time. No little kids running around them… kids. Alexandria would want those. And he happened to look up to where they were walking. His future wife was walking straight to Emma.

Emma was still fascinated with the fountains. She and Orry were marveling how they did it and he was explaining in great detail exactly how. Patrick and Alexandria came up behind them. He touched Emma on the shoulder and she flinched.

Vega saw it and so did Mac. Daniel moved slightly towards her. His father stopped him.

"Boss, think I'll take a walk over there. Your wife looks just a little uneasy." Mac was gone just like that to protect what was his Don's.

Vega leaned back on the limo. Daniel stood next to him… with security very evident around him.

"She could be you daughter, Sir," commented Daniel and he changed the subject as he realized that wasn't the brightest thing he ever said.

"She could, but she's not… thank God. Let's join them."

The Don and quite possibly the future Don ambled to join the party.

"Everything alright, Emmy? Tired yet?" asked her husband, sliding his arms round her shoulders.

"I'm fine, Philip. Would love some ice-cream though, and maybe some chocolate." She laughed; even she knew now for certain that she was pregnant.

"Ice-cream stand right there." Daniel pointed to it.

Philip nodded his head to Daniel. "Take her over to it, Daniel. Mikey," and he inclined his head at Mikey like an order without the rest of the words.

"So, Alexandria. You enjoying yourself in Vegas? We haven't had much time to talk since we arrived. Your mother looks well and so do you." He never mentioned Felicia, nor did he intend to. But Alexandria did.

"I am fine, Don Andrea. My mother and my sister send their best to you and said to thank you for the dinner last night. Mother is going home tomorrow. She doesn't like to be away from the vineyard too long and Felicia will fly on to Switzerland next week to visit friends. I am sure they will see you before they depart." Alexandria was doing her best to skirt around the topics and she was doing well.

Philip noticed how pretty she was. Still sweet and gentle unlike her sister. Emma was right. She would make a fine wife for his son and they would produce fine grandchildren. That was in the real world and this wasn't the real world.

Patrick stood dutifully by her. He didn't deserve her. Damn. Philip had pushed this. His thoughts were disturbed by Emma and Daniel returning, laughing and carrying ice creams for all, with some of the delicious ice cream stuck on her nose from the cone. Even Mikey was pulled into the venture with snacks of chips and chocolate also purchased there. But it broke the tension.

Philip made them all eat the ice cream outside of the Wynn's limos. Chocolate and chips were okay inside and there was water already in the cars. Just before they boarded the cars to do some more touring, Vega took Mac off to one side to talk. Mikey joined them.

"I think," and Vega took in the air, "we need to keep Patrick and Emma apart. I was hoping that it would work itself out, but it's not going to. I told her I know he made a pass at her and tonight I will ask her how much of one... and we will take it from there."

"Right, boss. Mikey will make sure that happens, right, Mikey?"

"You got it. Consider it done, boss." He turned away and left for the limo. Not a man to argue with.

"Mikey is tough, boss… Patrick gets out of line with him, he will regret it. You think we are still right?"

"I do. I keep getting this feeling we are being watched, and I also have this feeling that something is going to happen here in Vegas. Felicia worries me. Her hate is way too much. It was years ago when she and I were together, and she didn't see me end her brother. She knows it, but she didn't see it. She positively hates Emma. Make sure that you or I are with her at all times." He shivered in the warm sun. He even had the feeling in the suite. He was sure he personally was being watched… and Mac felt the same.

Chapter 24

The afternoon was fun. They drove; they shopped, ate lunch, viewed the sites, swapped old stories, made new stories, and generally had a great time, arriving back at the hotel with time to change before dinner. Still Philip and Mac had that feeling... so Mac searched the room again. He happened to brush against the flowers and they fell to the floor... and there it was, large as life. A camera. A very tiny one, hidden. Mac picked it out and disconnected it. He slipped it into his pocket and waited till Vega was on his own.

Emma was talking to Daniel in the lounge and Mac motioned his boss to step into the bedroom.

"Found it, boss. It was in the flowers. I'm sorry I missed it," and he reached in his jeans pocket and retrieved the tiny camera.

"Good God. I'm surprised you ever found it. How the hell did it get in there? Better still by whom? Someone must have wanted something to do at bedtime!" Vega thought about all the sex they had seen through it. "My God," he murmured. "I hope they didn't record it..."

"Good point, boss..."

Just then Emma came into the bedroom and saw Philip trying to hide something.

"What's in your hand, Philip?" Her expression intent on finding out.

No good lying to her. "A camera, babe... someone wanted to copy us having sex."

"What?!" she exclaimed not hiding her feelings.

"Seems that way," and he cut his eyes to Mac. He handed it back to him. "See what you can find out about this. I doubt the hotel knows anything about it. A feeling that it came from one of our party! We know all our own security."

"You are joking, Philip, right?" Emma asked, very perturbed at who had been watching and what they saw.

"I wish I was, baby. But someone saw a whole lot of us…" and his voice trailed off. The flowers had been directly opposite his side of the bed. "Jesus Christ," and he thought of Emma and the champagne sex they had enjoyed. But he also thought about what they had discussed between them. Vega told his wife nearly everything. Did they hear him telling her about the dream? That made him angry. "Fuck! Why didn't they just take binoculars and watch us…" and he thought, maybe they had. "Shut the curtains, Mac, now!"

Mac did it immediately. The same penny dropped with him.

"One way to find out who it is… Emma and I shared something no one else knows about, not even you, Mac. Maybe time to find out who else knows."

"You want me to wait outside for you, Mr. Vega?"

"Yeah, why don't you. Emma and I will get changed and we'll all go for dinner. And, Mac. This camera thing is our secret, and while we are at secrets there is something else I am going to share in the next day or two. Something I should have shared way back… didn't seem necessary but maybe now it does. Mac, it involves you and me. Tonight will probably be the last time we all have dinner together as a family…if my thoughts are right. Mac, did you say something to Patrick today?"

"I did. I told him that if he was your choice… we would not follow him!"

"And that stands no matter what?" Vega looked at his number one.

"It stands, boss. He has no respect for you and certainly none for your wife."

"What if he marries Alexandria?" asked Vega, sitting down on the side of the bed, sliding out of his shirt and pulling off his boots.

"I doubt it will make a difference. But it's your call, Sir. You are the Don and you have the final say."

"I do. Maybe you all should remember that."

"Yes, Sir, but we still will not work for him. For you, Don Andrea, we would die for. And you and I share something more than just friendship and loyalty, we have little Andrea."

It gave Vega the opening he needed.

"Mac, sit down. Emma please stay. What I have to say concerns you both. I was waiting till we were home but now is as good a time as any." Philip paced the room as he spoke.

He turned and looked at them both to see if they were seated. They were and his wife looked almost uncomfortable. She figured he was going to bring up the issue of Patrick right now.

"Emma…I know you think it's about Patrick, but it's not. You and I will discuss that on our own. I have Mac's story of what he saw and you are in no way to blame and I never thought you were. Later, baby, when you and I are alone." He smiled a warm and rich smile at her and then he began. "As you both know, Andrea is mine and Mac's grandchild." He smiled to himself. He had a grandchild and here he was producing more babies himself. He continued. "What you don't know, either of you…" he stopped and looked more at Mac. "Pauli married Donna at my request the day they were shot."

Emma stared at her husband not having any clue what to say.

Mac stood up from the bed and walked to the window. He seemed to stare there for minutes.

"I did it for my daughter's protection. I knew Pauli would look out for her. I didn't bank on him ending up dead…or Donna. As Emma knows, I have been dreaming about it a lot lately. The beach and finding them. Only Alex and Charlie know what we found there. It was carnage…" he stopped as he tried to compose himself. The memory was almost too much for him.

Vega turned away so neither of them saw tears in his eyes. Emma wanted to run to him and hold him tight, but she thought maybe there was more and she was right.

"Donna married him without question to give her baby a real name. Oh, he's a Vega through and through and he will still be raised as such. Donna was a Vega." He looked at Mac, who didn't offer any protest. "She did it for me. She really was in love with me and I should have told her who she was, but I think it would have broken her heart. It was bad enough she got pregnant the way she did…and Mac, it still bothers me that I shot and killed your son, a man we both raised. But better me than you. To kill one's own son is not a good thing to do…" and Patrick flashed through his brain, knowing that if his son laid another hand on Emma he would be finding that out. He continued. "Pauli was like my brother even more than Damien ever was. We shared so much and I trusted him with my daughter's life until Rossi took it away. Rossi always thought my step-brother should have been the Don…but that's in the past. What I do think now is that somehow one or more of my children is involved in this what ever you want to call it. And, I think I know who! But now is not the time to say."

Chapter 25

Now it was time for Emma to get up and go to her husband. "Philip, I would rather tell you in front of Mac what happened with Patrick. I know this isn't the best time for you, but it might be the best time for me. I don't know what Mac told you, but you will know for yourself that I am telling you the truth."

"Baby, I don't ever doubt you. You are the only one in my family I totally trust," and Vega pulled her to him and kissed her mouth very gently. "If you want to say it in front of Mac that's fine, but there really is no need."

"There is, Philip, because it's not the first time."

She felt him tense against her.

"What?!" and Vega was immediately angry.

Mac stepped in. No wonder she wanted to tell him in front of a witness. "Boss, sit down. Let her explain." And Mac moved towards him. He had the feeling that if Patrick was out there now Vega would take him himself.

"Please, Philip. Do what Mac asks you." She was trying hard to control her own emotions. Vega had just told them that Donna had married Pauli. She didn't even know what Pauli's last name was, only he was Philip's best friend in life. His daughter and friend and now this.

Philip moved to the large chair near the window and sat down in it. He crossed his legs and rested his hands under is face, and leaned on the arms of the chair, his eyes pin points of anger.

"Did Mac witness both?" was the only words Vega uttered.

"She told me the first time, boss. I was coming to you, but decided to see if it happened again, not that I didn't believe your wife, I wanted to catch him myself."

Vega's glare switched from one to the other.

"How long?" was all he murmured.

"Two weeks. First time I thought he was joking. Just playing around so I didn't even pay attention. He was drinking, just like you were…" she stopped, minding what she said.

"Like me…that's what you were going to say. Except I don't make advances to married women!" That wasn't true. Emma had been married when Philip stole her from her husband. He corrected himself. "Except you, babe."

Vega's cell rang. He ignored it. It rang again. Again, he ignored it.

She continued, very nervously. Her husband was now Don Andrea. Mac stood to the side of his chair just like he did at home. She almost felt like she was on trial. Thank God she was married to the man.

"I was in the nursery with the kids and Patrick said he came to help. He picked up Andrea and I thought a bit too heavy-handed. I took him from Patrick and as he handed him to me he touched my back leaving his hands there way longer than he should. I didn't think too much about it until the day before his birthday."

"Emma, stop right there. You should have come to me then or, if not me, then Mac. My son is not allowed to touch you and certainly he will not come near you again…ever!" Vega stood up and moved to the side of the bed. There was a bottle of scotch and a glass from earlier. He poured himself a drink. A drink that spelled trouble.

Mac raised his eyebrows to Emma and then looked at Vega. "You want me to deal with him, Sir?"

"Not yet. I want to know the last part." He nursed the glass, slowly turning it like he was crushing someone's neck between his hands. "Go on, Emma." He could sense her fear as she looked from him to Mac. "I'm not going to bite you," and he realized he was being the Don to his own wife. He curbed it a little. "Em, we have to know. I think that Patrick is part of what is going down here."

"Patrick?"

"Patrick…" and Philip waited for her to continue.

"I was in the kitchen the evening before his birthday, just fixing something to eat. You had gone upstairs to say goodnight to the children in the nursery and I was about to follow you. He came up behind me, slid his arms round my waist and kissed my neck… Mac was coming into the kitchen and Patrick let go immediately, so fast that I wasn't sure that Mac had seen him." Her speech was stopped as Vega threw the glass and its contents at the extra large window of the best suite in Wynn's hotel. The glass broke but the window didn't, proving it was more than likely bullet proof.

The suite door opened and Mikey appeared, gun in hand. Mac waved him back and he closed the door discreetly.

Emma didn't think she had ever seen Philip this angry. She could see the veins standing out on his neck. He called Mac to him and whispered in a deep, rough voice to him. She couldn't hear what he said, but a couple of sentences seemed to be in Italian. She didn't know Mac knew Italian, but she wished she had taken Daniel up on learning it.

She heard Patrick's name once or twice and as suddenly as the conversation started it stopped. Mac turned and looked at her.

"Mrs. Vega," and Mac moved to the door and left the room.

Emma had no idea what to expect as her husband turned to face her. She was still in her clothes from the day while Philip just was clad in jeans, not having time to shower before dinner.

"Emma, I am not angry with you, not one bit. I wish you had told me before the party, but I do understand loyalty and that's something you have. He is my son and you knew how unhappy I would be. I also understand he cannot be around you. It is tearing him apart… but that gives him no right to touch you or be near you ever again. He is the son I counted on, the one I trained, the one who was to take my place. He will not now or ever will. The Family will not work for him. I can only extend my apologies to you that you were treated like this. He will not be allowed back to the house. He will stay at the winery. Mac has gone to find him and Mikey will take care of the situation. Now you and I will shower and go to dinner." He reached his hand to her, but there was distance between them that wasn't there an hour ago.

Emma took his hand, but she knew things were changed. The Family Vega was changed for ever.

"Philip, I..."

Vega pulled her to him. He didn't wait for her approval or her consent. He wanted her there and then, perhaps just a little too much and it showed. He also knew that it was him that was supposed to be driving the Ferrari, him and Emma. Mac and his thoughts were right. Someone wanted them both out of the way and the family destroyed and that someone who was on the inside was the key. Was that someone Patrick? He thought about that. They were using Patrick to get to Philip and doing a good job about it. Tomorrow they would go home. It was time to find out and what better way than a sitting target... and aside from them that target was a five-year-old little boy named Andrea and a marriage certificate that needed to be found. There was a letter that went with it stating that the baby be brought up with Don Andrea. And a letter that proved who Pauli really was.

Chapter 26

When they returned from the shower, Philip remembered his cell calls. He hadn't been so gentle with her in the shower. His need was great. He sat on the end of the bed, just clad in a towel, which was tied around his waist. Vega looked at his phone. Two calls and a third while he was making love to his wife... all from Patrick.

"What the fuck? He got married! Boy has a conscience after all. Emma, come here!"

Emma almost fell out of the bathroom, half naked and hair still wet. She pulled a towel round her trim body.

"Who got married?" She was trying to dry her hair at the same time.

"Patrick!"

"What? Tonight?" She dropped the one towel.

"Yes, after we left them. Wants to meet up and have dinner as they are leaving for the winery first thing after breakfast. All of that family. Best thing he could have done."

Emma thought so, too. She was glad. She wouldn't have to worry about unwanted advances anymore.

Vega looked at his wife. "How do you feel about going to dinner, baby? It's your call. If we do go though, I would ask you wear what I pick out for you." There was a gleam in his eye and he went to the closet and opened the doors.

Emma didn't answer. She just watched him. He picked out the shortest skirt he could find and a top that matched, both jet black and sequins adorned the top, what there was of it. No room for anything under it, it would fit where it touched. Then he picked the shoes. High heels... gold, which matched the sequins.

"And, pray, what will you be wearing?"

"The tightest black jeans I have here and a black shirt open to the waist. I will instruct the twins to wear similar. You want to go?"

"Yeah, I want to go... I am not scared of your son! And I am your wife amongst other things..." and she laughed. She knew what her husband was doing.

And so they dressed for dinner. A Don and his mistress, lover, wife... any word that came to mind. It was to prove a point.

They stepped out of the bedroom into the lounge, Philip holding his wife's hand. He looked every inch a Don, shades, all in black, gun in the back of his jeans, and Emma, his woman and clearly so, legs up to her neck that met long dangling gold earrings and a lot more makeup than usual. If Patrick passed this test it wasn't him. If he didn't then he was done.

Mac and Mikey could not stop staring at their boss's wife. And the twins were shocked. This was their step-mother..............

"My God, dad... where did you find her? Wherever, I want one..." Daniel's admiration was apparent and even Orry was staring like he had never seen her before.

"Everyone ready. And stop staring at my wife like that!"

"Boss, I think the whole place is going to be looking at her like that..." Penny dropped. "That's the point, right?"

"Right..." and Philip clicked his fingers in a gun shape. "So you all heard? Patrick got married this evening... You didn't tell them, Mac?"

"Thought you would want that pleasure, Don Andrea." Mac replied, while moving to the door and calling for the elevator.

Vega smirked. "He's invited us all to dinner. His new family and us. So I am bringing my new wife, too." He purposely didn't mention about Pauli and Donna. This was not the time or the place. One bombshell at a time.

Daniel thought how smart his father was. Mac knew how smart Daniel's father was. And they took the elevator down to the lower floor and left for the dining room.

The said room was resplendent looking, even more exotic than last night. The chandeliers positively glistened and waiters hustled and bustled between tables moving once more out of the way for the incoming party.

And Philip saw his son and his new wife and he felt something. He wasn't quite sure what. He hoped he would make a go of it, make the girl happy. He, himself, certainly had not made her sister happy. He looked at Felicia. She was dressed to the hilt. Money dripping from her and there was his own wife, with barely any clothes on, but with a charm and innocence that Felicia could never achieve. Vega squeezed Emma's hand tightly trying to tell why he had made her dress this way, but she already knew.

Emma could have passed for twenty-one not thirty-one.

Patrick stood up from the table and greeted his father.

"I tried to call you to come to the wedding chapel. I could not reach you, Sir."

"I missed your calls. You are leaving first thing in the morning, I gather, for your new home. I'll have your car and clothes sent to you. Best, I think, that you don't come home for a while. Let the dust settle."

"You know, don't you?" and Patrick had to ask.

"I know what, Patrick?"

His son looked at Emma. A family he could once have inherited if he hadn't let lust get in his way. Vega had asked him to look after his family if anything happened to him.

Patrick looked at Emma, an overwhelming sadness deep in his eyes.

"I beg your forgiveness, Emma. I know I will never be the Don," and he turned to look at his father, one who would never quit his role. "Father, forgive me," and Patrick bent down and kissed his father's ring.

"Not sure I can, Patrick. Yours was the power and the glory, and now it goes elsewhere. Your brother will be *made* when he is sixteen and I will groom him in your place. You made the biggest mistake of all in pursuing my wife. But now we will honor your new bride. We will drink and dine with you, celebrate your new life. But only one of us gets to take home the prize." Vega could not have rubbed the fact in more if he had tried, and all but pulled Emma into the picture.

But Vega knew by the looks that passed between them and the words his son spoke he was involved in the events of the last few days. Patrick had been the advance party, only he took it one step too far. Had he put the camera in the bedroom? Quite possibly. He had the opportunity to, but even Vega doubted that his son was sick enough to watch them having sex, and last night he had been with Alexandria. He thought that maybe they were looking for pillow talk rather than pages from the Kama Sutra. Now he was trying to get out of the plan, but he was too far in. Mac had told him the family was not loyal to him… and that's where Charlie Hill came in. Charlie was on a mission for Vega.

They dined on traditional Italian food. They drank wine, except for Philip, who drank scotch and a lot of it. When his wife crossed her legs he rested his hands there and made no secret of the way he felt about her. Once or twice he called Mac to him and gave him an order. Vega was showing his son what he was about to miss.

And the woman he would never have.

At last he toasted his son. It was done with a tinge of sorrow. Again, it was to be the second son. Alexandria was radiant and happy as she looked at her new husband. Felicia could have killed Vega with the looks she gave him, and their mother was overjoyed at having Patrick as her son-in-law. At last there would be a man in the house. Someone to oversee the vineyard.

But Vega knew there was a traitor amongst them. Someone was watching them and had been coaching his son. Someone now had footage of he and Emma. And that someone had to be found. Was his son safe? Or had he sent him into the lion's den? On that he wasn't sure.

Chapter 27

Dinner was done. Emma seemed more relaxed.
Patrick asked his new bride to dance with him. Philip asked
Felicia to dance with him. Emma looked staggered. So did the rest of
the table. Felicia accepted. Vega whispered in Emma's ear and then to
Daniel before he left the table.

Philip took Felicia's hand and led her to the dance floor. He held
her in his arms rubbing in the fact that he was not hers. He held her
close and he talked to her very calmly and strongly, his face not giving anything away.

"Emma, Emma," would you like to dance with me?" asked the
second-born son.

"I would, thank you." Emma was almost shaking.

Mac pulled her chair out for her. "He's doing it for a reason,
Emma," Mac whispered.

And Emma looked back at Mac, a look of betrayal on her face.
She walked with Daniel to the dance floor and looked straight at her
husband, then looked away. Daniel took her in his arms, very strong
arms just like his father.

"It's for a reason, Emma. He's telling her to stay away from Patrick and Alexandria and, most of all, himself and you. He will warn
her only once…"

"And then what, Daniel… he'll blow her away like he does the
others…"

"Emma, he has to protect what is his, including you…" Daniel
protested.

Tears streamed down her face. She didn't know till that moment how jealous she could be.

"Emma, don't let them see you crying. Come on lets go get a drink or something. Please, Emma. Don't let my father see you…"

"Let's go," and they left the floor to go to the bar, with Mikey close behind them.

Vega watched them and he knew he had hurt his wife. He had whispered to her, but maybe she didn't catch what he meant. Still he kept hold of Felicia, and still he told her what not to do. But his eyes watched his wife and where she went to.

At the bar she ordered a double vodka and then another. She never drank vodka. Tonight she did. Daniel had a scotch. Mikey got it for him, and Mikey stood close by.

Emma drank it down. It was bitter. They put the drinks on the Vega suite number. Mikey had an orange juice. Emma couldn't watch anymore. She wanted her room.

She slid down from the barstool she had been sitting on, her skirt now extremely short and attracting more of a fair share of lookers until Mikey stepped up.

"Mrs. Vega, let's get you upstairs. Daniel," and Mikey led the way to the elevator and up to the suite, leaving Mac with the rest of the party.

"Emma must not be feeling well," commented Mac. "When Mr. Vega returns we should say goodnight."

And Mr. Vega did return with Felicia, Patrick and Alexandria in tow. He was courteous. "I bid you all goodnight. Patrick, once more I congratulate you. Walk with me to the elevator." And all but dipped his head to the ladies at the table.

Father and son walked to the elevator in complete silence. Once there Vega hugged his son to him by placing his hands on his son's shoulders.

In Patrick's ear, he spoke the words that Patrick would never forget.

"You are my first-born son. You were the chosen one. You had it all. I love you dearly… but if you ever touch my wife again, you are dead!" And he kissed him on each cheek and walked away, climbing into the waiting elevator.

Patrick stood there trying to compose himself. He had to get out of this now, before it went any further. It was all wrong, all of it. He knew that his father suspected it was more than just touching Emma. Much more. It was his father's job to know. And now there was no way back. When his partners found out that Vega knew he was in on it, he was probably dead.

Mac accompanied his boss to the suite.

Daniel and Mikey sat waiting.

"Patrick won't be back for a long time and Felicia won't give us any more trouble." Philip looked around. "Where is Emma?"

Daniel looked towards the bedroom door.

Vega went to the door and tried the handle. It was locked.

"Emma, open the door. Emma, do you hear me, open the door, baby."

No reply.

"Emma, are you okay in there? Emma, open the God damn door, now!"

Still no reply.

"She was upset, Sir. She didn't understand why you danced with Felicia. And she drank vodka." Mikey added almost ashamed.

"You let her? She's pregnant. She doesn't get to drink vodka! Emma, God damn it, unlock the door." All Vega heard was silence. "Mac, get a bedroom door key up here, now!"

"Boss, you can get in through the massage room door..." He, too, was concerned for Emma, but not for the same reason her husband was.

Vega took off through the other door, into the massage room and through to the bedroom. There he found Emma sitting on the bed, tears streaming down her face, her legs pulled up to her chin, and all she had on was lace panties and the black top.

"What the hell is wrong, baby? Why didn't you open the door to me?" he made the mistake of moving towards the bed and to her.

She screamed at him. "Get away from me!" as she leapt from the bed and ran into the bathroom trying to shut the door behind her to keep him away from her.

"Emma, what the fuck is wrong with you? You're drunk!" And he pushed the door hard that she was trying to close on him. He was much stronger than she was and pushed her almost into the wall of the bathroom.

They could be heard from the lounge and Mac was more than concerned for her and for his boss's safety. Vega was carrying.

Mac yelled into the bathroom. "Mr. Vega, are you okay in there? She doesn't understand, boss. All she saw was you holding Felicia. She doesn't know why." His voice was loud trying to attract Vega's attention.

"I don't care what she thinks she saw. I am fighting for this family and this is ridiculous… she's drunk, and you people let her get this way," as he moved even closer to her.

All they heard was her scream and a very loud slap across Vega's face. "Go back to your girlfriend! I don't want you!"

And without even thinking what he was doing he raised his hand to her just as Mac burst though the door.

"Boss, no…!" and he tried to grab Vega's arm.

It was too late. He hit her, something he had never done, not to any woman. Vega hit his own wife.

Chapter 28

Emma slumped to the floor in total shock. Philip had hit her, but it did sober her up very fast, and if she was honest she deserved it. She had hit him first.

Mac stared at Vega. "Boss…"

"I didn't mean to hit her… it was instinct. Oh, my God…" and Philip turned from the room afraid of his own strength. "Help her, Mac." And he fled from the bedroom and into the lounge. He didn't even wait for Mikey as he left the suite in a great hurry, complete with gun.

Mikey yelled to the security to follow their boss, at least two of them. Vega dived into the elevator and left before anyone could catch him. He was gone out of the hotel and into the street. He hailed a cab that would take him anywhere on the cash he had on him… all the way back to Los Angeles if he wished. All he had on him aside from cash, was his ID and his gun… and he sported shame. He leaned back on the leather seating that had tears in it.

"Where to, Sir," asked the driver, half turning to look at his passenger and realizing this was no ordinary fare. Maybe some kind of hit man.

"Anywhere. Just drive!"

"Yes, Sir," and the cabbie pulled out into the oncoming late night traffic and drove.

Vega thought back to what he had done. He had hit her. The night's events were no excuse, but it was all backing up on him. Suddenly, a church appeared ahead of him, big spires loomed out like fingers pointing to him in the darkness… beckoning him.

"Stop right there, by the church…" Philip had no clue where he was. "Pull over. Wait for me. Here is a hundred to hold you. If you wait, there is another hundred in it for you plus a tip."

"Yes, Sir," and he stretched the bill that Vega handed to him. It was real. "I'll be here, Sir," and the cabbie pulled into the almost deserted parking lot of the Catholic Church and let his passenger out. His sign was off, and Mr. Cabbie rested back in his seat and waited.

Philip Vega walked up the church steps of the old and sprawling church and pushed open the massive wooden door. It groaned under its own weight. His eyes immediately caught the statue of the Virgin Mary and he crossed himself. He walked slowly up through the rows of seating till he reached the first row. He sat down in the pew and dropped his head into his hands… as the tears flowed.

So involved in his own sorrow he didn't hear the priest enter the church and come down the pew to him. Vega looked up, his eyes red and wearing his soul on his sleeve.

"My Son… welcome to God's House…" and the priest sat down next to Vega.

"Father, I need forgiveness…" and Philip Vega, master of all and subservient to no one, was a broken man.

Father Murphy looked at this man next to him. Not an ordinary man. Expensive clothes, and noting the gun in the back of his jeans as he approached him. Obviously very wealthy and most probably a family man. A hit man? Maybe? More than likely a Boss.

The Father crossed himself and spoke softly to Vega.

"You feel the need for a gun in the House of God, my son?"

"I feel the need of it to stay alive, Father!" and Philip looked at the man he called Father. He was early thirties in age, but worldly wise in experience.

"You are not from here, my son?"

"Los Angeles."

"City of Angels."

"Yeah, right. More like city of demons!"

"You have demons, my Son?"

Vega looked straight into the face of the priest. "I have a vice, an obsession. Her name is Emma. She is my wife and the chink in my armor."

"And in your profession that is not good?" Father Murphy lowered his voice.

"Is it good in any profession? But to answer your question, no, it's not." Vega paused. "You know what I am?"

"I have a good idea, my Son. You carry a gun. And you are obviously wealthy, and too wealthy for a hit man… therefore I think you are a Boss and probably a very powerful one from Los Angeles. A Don, maybe?"

"That obvious… and one who tonight denied his son and hit his wife… there is so much more, Father." Tears streamed down Vega's face. "Not becoming to a Don, is it?"

"That's what I am here for, Sir, to hear your confessions. Maybe not so becoming to a Don, but it is to a man that so obviously loves his wife, or he would not be sitting here."

Vega smiled through his pain.

"There is more, my Son, is there not?" Father Murphy toyed with his rosary and Vega's eyes were drawn to it like a magnet.

Vega opened up to the priest in a full confession. His son, his wife, Pauli, his daughters… mostly his downfall for the love of his wife and how he had stolen her from someone else, because he loved her, and he wanted her, and what he wanted, he got… and Pauli, who was not just his friend, but whose last name was also Vega.

Philip Vega was there for an hour, and the clock ticked by to midnight. He wondered if the cabbie was still outside. He sincerely hoped so as he had no clue where he was or how to get home. He could call Mac, but for some reason he didn't want to. Philip thought about just not going back there tonight. He had disgraced the Vega name. He didn't need his son to do it. He had managed it all on his own.

Finally he stepped out into the cool night air. He had thanked the Priest for listening and helping, as the Father had followed him to the door, where Vega left a considerable contribution to the church fund.

"Don Andrea, I have a feeling I will see you again. Maybe come back sometime and bring your wife. She must be a very special woman for you to love her so much. But remember she must love you very much to take on your lifestyle, your family and give you five children. You are a very lucky man," and Father Murphy closed the heavy wooden doors for the night.

Vega headed for the cab which was still waiting. As he did, his cell rang. He looked at the number. It was Mac.

Vega hesitated. "Yeah?"

"Where the hell are you, boss? We are worried sick about you. You have been gone for hours."

Vega noticed he said we. He didn't say Emma.

"I have no clue where I am, but I am fine." He paused very noticeably. "And my wife? She miss me, too?"

"She's going frantic, boss. It was her idea to call you. She needs you very badly right now. She's a lost soul, just like when you found her. She thought you were leaving her!"

Chapter 29

Emma grabbed Mac's cell. "Philip, please don't leave me! Don't ever leave me!" she was begging him, the only way she knew how. Whatever it took to keep him, she would do.

"Baby... I hit you. How can you want me...?"

"I hit you, too... I should not have done that. I should have believed that you were doing what you had to do with her. Mac told me all about it. But when I saw you out there on the dance floor with Felicia... I couldn't handle it. Oh, God, Philip, I need you." Her voice broke up on the cell. She was crying. "Please come home."

As she spoke he was climbing into the cab.

She heard him say Wynns.

"Baby, put Mac back on the phone. I'll be home shortly."

Vega waited for Mac to collect the phone again. "Boss?"

"Tell me she didn't lose the baby..."

There was silence.

"Mac... did she?" There was severe anguish in his voice and he stared at the glass in the windows of the cab.

"Damn near, boss. She was hysterical. I put her in the shower, me, boss, no one else. Scrubbed her clean of makeup and vomit. She has a black eye from where you hit her. But, no, she didn't lose it. How is your face?"

"Haven't looked. Been in a church the whole time." He looked again in the window. He had a bruised face also. "I'm on my way back. Be there in about twenty minutes. Mac, I denied Patrick to be Don and told him if he touched my wife ever again... he is dead! I told him before I came back to the suite," and he cut the call off.

Vega leaned back in the seat. It started to rain, big drops rolled down the windowpane.

"I waited, boss, just like you asked." The cabbie was proud of himself and he wanted the money.

"You did." Vega pulled money from his back pocket. "What's your name?" And he reached over and gave the guy an additional three hundred in hundred dollar bills.

"Vinnie, boss. Driving cabs isn't all I do, Sir," and he set the windshield wipers in motion.

Vega had figured that for himself. "I gathered that. You know folks round here, Vinnie?"

"I do. Sir, are you from Los Angeles, boss?"

"I am. Vinnie do you know me somehow? Know who I am?"

"I know you must be a Boss, Sir. You came from Wynns. Only wealth and movie stars come from Wynns. I think you are both, Sir. Are you the movie star Philip Vega?"

Philip was shocked. Vinnie was implying both.

"I am. Your next line will be: you've seen all my films."

"No, Sir, but I do know of your Family! Well respected even up here. You want anything done here, you call me," and Vinnie handed his card over the seat to Vega.

"I'll keep that in mind, Vinnie. Indeed, I will."

"We are here, Mr. Vega. Remember, I am at your service." Vinnie pulled into the cab zone at Wynns, taking less than fifteen minutes to return home.

"I'll remember," and Vega jumped out of the cab into the pouring rains of Las Vegas. Kinda of fitted the mood.

The doorman was quick to open the door, but it didn't stop Vega from getting wet, his shirt soaked straight through and water running down his hair. Only his jeans were spared any lasting damage.

Philip took the elevator up to the suite, not quite knowing what he was walking into. It stopped and the door opened to security everywhere. He crossed into the lounge and the first thing he saw was Emma. She sat on the couch, legs curled under her like a little lost child. A giant white robe swamped her, and her hair was pulled back in a pony tail clearly showing her black eye. To each side of her, like bookends, sat the twins. Daniel had his arm round her shoulders taking charge of her.

Mac had been fixing a drink and set it straight down when his boss appeared.

"Don Andrea," and Mac moved forward to acknowledge his boss.

Mikey dipped his head to Vega in a sign of respect.

Philip wondered what they were really thinking of him striking his own wife. He looked back to Emma, whose face was both puffy from crying and from his blow.

"I..." and that's as far as he got with his intended speech.

Emma jumped up from the couch, the large robe engulfing her and she ran to her husband, throwing her arms round him, wet shirt not stopping her. He cradled her in his arms and his head dropped onto her hair as he whispered to her how sorry he was. He ran his hand through her hair and pulled the band from it, hugging her even tighter if that was possible, and kissing her waiting lips.

"Maybe we should leave you two alone..." Mac looked at them and then looked at the floor. "You know, so you can compare bruises..."

Vega smiled. "I need you all to stay. There is something I have to tell you... all of you..." he paused. "Emmy, then you and I will take a day here, just for the two of us... do whatever you want to do, while you guys get lost for the day..."

"You need something dry, boss?"

"Grab me anything, Mac," and he let go of Emma for just a second, and peeled off his wet shirt. His bruised chest and his scar could still be seen, and now the one on his face added color.

"Not sure which one of you looks the prettiest now, Emma. You or Dad..." and Orry laughed at his own joke and gained new respect from Daniel.

Vega looked at his sons, ones he was very proud of.

Mac arrived back in time for the end of the joke carrying a black robe for his boss plus a towel.

"Thanks, Mac," and handed him the wet shirt. He towel-dried his hair and slipped the robe on, then sat himself down on the biggest couch near the door and pulled Emma with him. "Mac..."

That was Mac's cue for a scotch, even at this hour. It was now way passed midnight, but this had to be told now before Vega lost his courage. He drank the scotch down in one go and set the glass down, and then he stood up feeling it would give him the advantage. He paced the room a little.

"Tonight I spent time with a Priest. My first confession in years. But there was a lot I had to confess to," and he glanced at his wife. "You, Emma, were the first thing. You thought I had betrayed you. I have not nor ever will. I love you too much for that and would give my life for you." He looked away, emotions overwhelming him. He faltered just slightly. "I told my eldest son if he ever touches my wife again, he is dead! And that stands. Daniel…"

And Daniel looked at this man that commanded so much respect and honor.

"You will be *made* on your sixteenth birthday. You will be the next Don. And your children will follow you. Orry, I hope that does not offend you…"

"Not in the least, Father. I am happy about your choice. Now I can do all the things Daniel can't," and he smiled at both his brother and father. "And I have plans for college. He will need a good attorney!"

Vega smiled at him as Daniel hit Orry playfully on his arm.

"But Daniel, one day there is someone who may contest you for the right, or contest your sons."

"Your other sons," joked Daniel, very lightheartedly. "I mean, you'll have enough of them."

But Vega didn't laugh back and he took a deep breath. "Not my son. A little boy who is only five. Mine and Mac's grandchild."

"How can that be, Sir… I know you gave him the name of Vega," stated Daniel, obviously shocked.

"Pauli was not just my friend… he was my cousin. That's why we were always together. My father had a sister who was Pauli's mother, and who never married, so his last name was Vega by law, and the little boy is legally Andrea Pauli Vega."

Chapter 30

There was dead silence until Mac broke the ice.

"Did Damien know?"

"No. My father kept it quiet... very quiet, for obvious reasons. He was ashamed that she had produced a son... a bastard. But he did make sure he was financially secure, and no, Pauli didn't know till he was older who he was. Pauli was always loyal to me every day of his life and I trusted him beyond question. When I asked him to take Donna and the baby he was right there, and only gave her back the name she already had. She was a Vega... I know the baby was Marc's son, but Donna earned the right and even if she hadn't when Pauli married her he gave her his name."

"Mind if I have a scotch, boss?" asked Mac.

"I think we could all use one, except my wife..." retorted Philip.

"Dad... does anyone else know?" asked Orry.

"Million dollar question, son. I think maybe they do. Emma and I talk about most things and Mac found a camera in the bedroom. And aside from doing what comes naturally in bedrooms, we talk a lot." He paused. "What you saw me telling Felicia last night was to leave my son alone. I could hardly tell her in front of Patrick and his new wife."

"You think she is involved?" asked Mac.

"I think maybe she is, and someone we haven't heard of for five years. Someone who would love to see both Emma and I dead... and little Andrea in our place."

"But who else would know, boss?" Mac was thinking hard.

"Someone who was there when Andrea was born. Was in the house and knew Rossi. Someone who sent Rossi to kill Pauli and Donna. But the baby escaped unhurt. I sent Charlie on a mission back at the house to find out if JJ has left Switzerland. Big coincidence that Felicia is headed there next week. Alexandria told me. I called home earlier. Alex has three men with him at all times in the nursery. The house is on full alert. They won't do anything until Emma and I are taken care of, and that isn't going to happen. That's why we are here and not at home. Tonight, on my own, I was a sitting target, and that was my fault. It was all just too much…"

Vega took the drink that Mac handed him. A double scotch.

"You need anything to eat, boss?"

"I'm fine. Well, maybe a sandwich or something if you can get one. I do need to talk to my wife and get some sleep, though. We can discuss this more in a few hours. Patrick and Alexandria will be gone at breakfast and the rest of that family. We can focus more then. Emma," and he offered her his hand, which she gladly accepted. Philip pulled her up from the couch and circled her with his arms. "Let's go, baby. Mac will bring us something to eat." He looked at his sons. "We'll meet about ten, for an hour, and then I want the rest of the day just with my wife. I have somewhere to take her, someone I want her to meet and this person would also like to meet her. He has heard so much about her." Vega laughed. "Let's go, babe… it's almost two, and I think we both need beauty sleep." He ushered her into the bedroom and left the door ajar for Mac.

Through the windows there was a zillion stars shining. Philip led her to the window, now knowing it was most certainly unbreakable glass, but noting the rain had stopped.

The stars reminded him of her ring. "Emma… will you marry me?"

"What? We are already married, Philip," and she giggled, pushing her hair out of his way as he leaned in to kiss her.

"I know we are. But we can renew our vows, right here in Vegas, in a beautiful church I found tonight. I repeat… will you marry me?"

She leaped into his arms. "Everyday of my life!" and Emma cried a ton of happy tears on his shoulder as he held her tightly to him. She slid down his body where her lips met his and he kissed like he would never let her go.

And outside the door Mac could hear them. Maybe the sandwich could wait and he pushed it into the open door and then closed it very gently.

Mac knew his boss needed her very much and he walked back into the room and sat down on the couch. Somehow he had always known that Pauli and Philip were extremely close, more than just friends. Vega never put Pauli in harms way. Always made sure he had the best of things. Nice car, the best room in the house after the family. Family... he had been family. Pauli was there before Mac was introduced to the family... he would have been forty-eight this year. Two years younger than both he and his boss. Mac leaned back on the couch and dozed a little. Someone had to look out for his boss even in the early hours and, generally, that someone was him.

He woke with a start and looked at his watch. Eight a.m. There was no sound from Vega's room. All he could hear was the phone ringing about three feet from him. He grabbed it so that it wouldn't wake the others.

"Yeah... Vega suite." He corrected himself.

"Mac... it's Charlie Hill. Andrea around?"

"Not awake yet. We all had a very late night, as in three a.m. this morning late. You want me to give him a message?"

"Ask him to call me when he wakes up. I have some news about JJ," and Charlie was gone.

Mac hung up the phone and was about to go to his room to take a quick shower.

"Phone ring, Mac?" A somewhat bleary eyed Vega appeared at the door wrapping his robe round him

"Don't you ever need sleep, boss?"

"Not often. Would you just sleep lying next to that young lady in there?"

"Good point. She still asleep?"

"She is... she needs it more than I do. Thanks for the sandwich. I just ate it. We should order some breakfast. So, who was on the phone? Charlie?"

"Yes, Sir... said he had news. You want to call him back? I can use the other phone to order breakfast. No sign of your sons yet or Mikey."

Vega moved to the phone and dialed. "Yeah. Would like to know what he found out, even though I have a pretty good idea already. I have a feeling that JJ is over here and not in Switzerland anymore. But she is not the central figure. Nor is Felicia. It's someone with more brains that put this together and that's what we have to find out. Felicia doesn't have that much to gain from this except revenge on me. JJ would love to see me dead. But there is someone else..." he stopped talking to Mac. "Thought you were never going to pick up the phone, Charlie. So what did you find out?" Vega listened. "Really? We will fly home tomorrow or maybe the next day at the latest. Good job, Charlie. Always rely on you. How's Jonas? Sorry to hear that. You should have stuck with Janine. She really liked you. Still does, I gather. Oh, she's way over me..." and Vega stopped... she was, but her father wasn't. The old Don was still alive and well. "Charlie... do me another favor. Check on Janine's father. See what he is up to nowadays. Someone with power is behind this... someone who could find out certain things."

The bedroom door opened, and a waif of a girl came through the open space. The robe still way too big and hair hanging down her face. Still, she was stunning even with the black eye. She rubbed her eyes. There wasn't a spec of makeup on her.

"Philip, I'm hungry... oh, and the doctor called my cell... It's official. We are having a baby... again..." and she laughed.

Vega now knew he would move heaven and hell to keep this family safe and Mac knew the same.

Chapter 31

"Charlie, I have to go. I have to look after my wife. She is offi-cially pregnant now... like none of us knew that." And Vega disconnected the call.

Philip picked Emma up like she weighed nothing, and held her in the air, half turning her round and then set her down. "Forgot about my damn ribs... Emma, let's eat and then I want to take you to church, the church we will renew our vows in. Won't take us long. Mac can come with us. The rest stay behind. We'll be back by lunch, have the meeting and then the rest of the day is our own." Vega had it planned out. "Mac, get Emma something to eat. I need to shower and make a call." And he was gone.

"Good job you can keep up with him, Emma."

"Sometimes, I can't. What did Charlie have to say?" she asked, while looking for something to drink. She found water at the bar and also some fruit there, too.

"Mac, I can eat this fruit, and there are crackers. Don't tell my husband, but I am not that hungry and both you and I know how clean I am," her laugh was precocious, as she pulled the robe tighter round her.

Mac knew why Vega loved her so much. But he didn't answer her question about Charlie.

Vega was only gone fifteen minutes, and came back in a darker mood than when he had left the room. He tried hard to hide it, but Emma knew his moods well.

"Ok, baby. Go and get dressed if you would. I already called for a cab. You have fifteen minutes to be ready. Your clothes are on the bed and I hope you don't mind that I picked them out for you. There is a reason."

Emma scurried away to the bedroom, glancing at her husband as she did. He was conservatively dressed in a grey Armani suit and high necked shirt.

"Mac, you have ten minutes to be ready, too. We have to go."

"Right, boss," and he left the room.

Philip made sure his cell was attached and his gun in the usual place in the back of his pants. He paced up and down while he waited. He drank a scotch. He drank another scotch. Nibbled on some of the crackers Emma had left, reminding himself to make sure she was eating properly which, right now, she wasn't.

Emma came through the door. He turned to look at her, starting at the bottom. The heels were high and expensive, and grey. Tanned, bare legs. The dress was short but tasteful, shaped and very slimming, capped neckline and just a tiny sleeve. He knew what she was wearing underneath. He had picked that out, too. Not too much makeup, enough to cover the bruise on her face and shades did the rest. Her hair hung down, which helped. Round her neck she wore a single cut diamond on a chain that matched her ring. She looked captivating and that was the idea.

"Perfection," he murmured.

She blushed.

He liked that she still did that.

"Mac," yelled Vega.

"Here, boss," and he appeared through the door also in a suit, and he stared at Emma.

Mac called for the elevator and the three took it down to the ground floor and the waiting cabbie, who was driving a town car, sleek, black and was more than luxurious to set the mood.

Vinnie was leaning on the side of the car and moved forward to open the door for Vega.

"Vinnie, this is my wife… Emma Vega."

"Wow…" he was looking her up and down. "Er, sorry, boss. You said she was something special. You didn't say she was drop-dead gorgeous." Vinnie was shocked. At first glance he thought she was

Vega's daughter.

Vega smiled. That she was...drop-dead gorgeous. He had turned the duckling into the swan. The swan had been there all the time. Just took the right man.

"Mrs. Vega…" and Vinnie held the door for her and her husband.

"And this is Mac. My personal bodyguard."

Vinnie looked at Mac and dipped his head. One bodyguard he didn't want to mess with.

"Same place as last night, Vinnie," announced Vega, as he leaned back on the smooth upholstery.

"Yes, Sir. You feel better this morning, boss? You sure look it…"

"Much, thank you." He glanced at Emma. She was the reason he felt better.

The drive wasn't far and Mac sat there as the passenger, not a luxury that he had very often.

The car pulled up outside the church and Father Murphy came down the steps to great his awaited visitors. His robes flowed behind him as he took the first few steps down to meet them. He was younger than most, but as Vega knew, full of knowledge.

The Priest put out his hand to great his new friend, and as he did, he dipped his head as a mark of respect for Vega's position in life.

"Father Murphy," and Vega ushered his wife in front of him. "This is Emma Vega, my wife."

"Mrs. Vega. It is my great pleasure to meet you. I heard a lot about you last night, and you are just as Don Andrea described you."

Vinnie smiled to himself. Right first time.

"I'll stay with the car, boss. Take your time," and Vinnie leaned back on the car's side and adjusted his gun in his jeans, letting it be known he was armed. His balding head was hidden by a cap today, but his jeans and leather jacket were similar to last night. He, too, wore shades, as did his fares.

Vega nodded to him and he, Emma and Mac followed the Priest up the steps into the church.

Emma stepped inside the church. It was stunning. There were flowers everywhere and a thousand candles gleamed in the church. Huge stain glass windows heralded the alter in front of them. She had never seen anything like it and it took her breath away. She walked a little way up the aisle and stopped, her heels clicking on the marble floors. Now she knew why Philip had asked to renew the vows here.

"Today? Now?" she asked her husband very excitedly.

"No, baby. In a week or so. I wanted you to see the church. Make sure you liked it. Father Murphy will make sure all the arrangements are made at this end and we will take care of the rest. I want all the family to be here and, besides, we have some things to sort out first… like who is trying to kill us."

"That's why you both carry guns in our church?" asked the Father.

"Mostly, Father. Someone wants to be rid of us." Vega could not tell the Father that this would be a good place for them to try. "And as you see, I have a lot to protect!"

Chapter 32

An hour at the church to make plans was all that was needed. Music, flowers and the service. Father Murphy was politeness itself, especially in front of a lady.

"You just name the date, Mr. Vega and God's house is your house." He turned to Emma. "You have children you want to bring?"

"We do. We have four and my husband has three others plus a grandchild." She didn't explain he was also Mac's grandchild, nor did she mention his daughter.

"We shall welcome them all. You just let me know when…" and he walked to the door with his new friends.

Once more Vega handed him money… This time in the form of a check that would cover the wedding and also build a new wing on a children's home that Father Murphy ran.

Emma stepped outside into the bright sunlight and there was Vinnie with the car. For one second she thought she saw a flash of light and she turned to tell Philip, but he was talking intently to the Father.

Mac turned to see where Emma was looking. He saw the flash and then it was gone.

"Emma… get in the car. I'll get Mr. Vega." Mac hurried back to his boss. "Mr. Vega, we should get going. You have calls to make."

Vega looked at him like he was nuts, but he happened to look at Emma, who was climbing quite hurriedly into the car. He took the hint.

"I will be in touch with you, Father."

"Good day, my son. I look forward to hearing from you." And the Father said his goodbyes.

Vega followed his wife and Vinnie held the door for him.

"Was it a gun?" asked Vega.

"No. I think it's binoculars. Someone is watching you both. Any ideas, boss?"

"Charlie has. Let's get to the hotel. I don't think we are in any harm here, not with three of us carrying. I think we are being tracked. We'll get something to eat and talk over the meal. I have some calls to make, also. Maybe we should fly home tonight or at least first thing in the morning. It's not us I am worried about, but the children." Vega fell silent and the car took them back to the hotel.

The car stopped. "Vinnie, pick us up at six. Me and Mac."

Emma looked at her husband.

"You stay with the twins and Mikey. I want to check something out. That's all Just something for the wedding." What he wanted to check out was security for when they went back to Vegas and he couldn't do that in front of his wife.

"Wynns…home of the wealthy," laughed Vinnie and climbed out and opened the door for the lady and her husband. "Six, boss."

And he was gone.

"I think the restaurant would be good. Then, Emma, a couple of hours in the private pool for you and I. Get you some more tan. Mac, get the twins down here and Mikey. Emma and I will get a table. We're fine." Vega moved his gun from the back to his hip, which was much more accessible.

Vega took her hand and led her into the restaurant. Instant power service was upon them and also the best table. Vega sat down with his back to the wall and the advantage of seeing the whole room, Emma right next to him.

"You look tired, baby. We'll lay by the pool and then you guys eat in the suite tonight. Mac and I won't be long. Just some business to take care of."

"I can't go with you?" she asked him.

"No, so please let it go."

She pouted.

"Won't work, babe." He sipped water from the ice cold glass full of it.

She leaned closer and whispered in his ear.

"Won't work either. I'd just take you," and he laughed. "You would give in to me anyway."

"No, I wouldn't!" and she pouted again.

He slid his hand under the table, onto her legs and just slightly inside the left leg and moved his hand higher.

She squirmed in her seat. He kept tight hold and raised his hand higher under her dress.

"Ok, you made your point. Someone will see you."

"Yeah, so... we're married." Vega thought it was funny.

"Philip, stop..." she was getting embarrassed.

"Why? Tell me it doesn't feel good," and he carried right on.

"That's the point. It feels very good," and her voice was low and sexy.

And Philip didn't want to stop and his hand ventured further till he subtly reached her black lace underwear. Thank God the table clothes hung long on the round tables.

He found what he was searching for.

"Philip..."

"Yeah, babe," and his voice was now on a different level.

"Philip... stop... please..."

"On one condition," he murmured, almost under the same spell she was. He whispered in her ear.

"Okay, Philip... right after lunch..." and she tried to look round her to see if anyone had noticed they were all but having sex right then and there in the restaurant. "Philip..."

He still had his hand on her thigh.

His eyes were staring straight ahead of him. He blinked. "What the hell is he doing here?"

Emma looked at where he was looking. There walking towards them was Patrick. Emma felt her husband's hand clench even harder round her thigh.

Vega's other hand went towards his gun... just in case.

Patrick approached them. "Sir, may I speak to you in private?"

"What the hell are you still doing here? I thought we had an agreement." Vega stopped speaking. And he almost gave away what he was thinking. "What ever you want to say you can say in front of *my* wife."

"Can I? You sure that's what you want?" Patrick frowned.

"I'm sure. Just say it." Vega's hand was still near his gun.

Patrick glanced across the table. It was obvious to any fool what was going on underneath the table cloth.

"Felicia and Alexandria are back at the winery with their mother. I am leaving here tonight and you will not see me again. But I wanted to talk with you in private without everyone around you. But I see that's not possible. Someone is following you. Where ever you go they go."

"So what's new… we know that. And what concern is it of yours? You have a new life, a wife and a winery to look after. So don't you think you better get and see to those things?" Vega was sharp with his son. He wasn't doing what he was supposed to be doing.

"I also wanted to tell you that Felicia is not going away next week."

"I knew that, too!" he paused. "Anything else before you leave us?" Vega was doing more talking with his eyes than his mouth.

Patrick looked at Emma. Her face was very flushed, but he could clearly see the bruising where someone had hit her and he had a good idea who, as his father sported the same kind of bruising on his face.

He paused, sheer contempt for his father. "Yeah, get a room!" and Patrick turned on his heal and walked away out of their lives.

Chapter 33

"**S**eemed my son is pissed at us. Wonder why?" and Vega smiled, almost smirked, like he was enjoying it, or there was some dark secret that only he knew about. He let go of his wife and picked up his ice water taking a long drink.

Emma watched him. Something was on his mind...something she was not privy to yet again. As she looked across the restaurant, she could see the rest of their group hurrying along to join them. Mac did not look happy.

He reached the table first. "Boss, what the hell was Patrick doing here?"

"Came to warn me that we are being followed and that Felicia is not going to Switzerland."

"We know that! That's all?" asked Mac.

"I doubt it!" Philip changed the subject. "Let's eat. I am starving and I know Emma is. Right, Em?" Philip was way too calm.

She just nodded. The whole event so far at lunch was too much for her to take in. Her husband was acting like nothing had happened. "Excuse me. I have to find a restroom," and she stood up before the others even sat down.

Philip knew exactly why she needed it. "Mikey."

And he was gone after her.

"Everything alright, boss?"

Vega cut his eyes at Mac. "We'll be leaving at six as planned tonight. First thing in the morning, we head home. Make sure the jet is ready."

"Always ready, boss." There was a puzzled look on his face.

Vega looked at his sons, who also seemed not to understand what was happening.

The waiters appeared to seat the party and also to take the orders.

"I'll order for Emma. She doesn't eat enough to keep a sparrow alive." He studied the menu.

The twins sat down and Daniel looked to Mac, who just shrugged his shoulders. This time he was lost.

"So you and Emma still going to the pool, boss?"

"Yes, any reason we shouldn't?"

"None at all. Boys and I will hang out in the casino. I'll teach them how to play poker… if they don't already know." Mac waited for a reaction. There wasn't one. Now he knew something was wrong.

Vega ordered steak for himself and a smaller one for Emma. He looked up from the menu. "Daniel, make sure she eats dinner, okay? She has two to feed."

"Yes, Sir," and he also picked steak.

Vega also ordered scotch and wine for Emma. An unusual choice for his wife. One glass would not hurt her. He allowed the twins wine also. He leaned back in his chair, oozing confidence, and a certain look that wasn't there a few hours ago.

Emma returned to her seat and Mikey pulled her chair out for her. She had been gone far longer than needed and Philip knew why.

"Everything okay, baby?" knowing full well why she took so long.

She whispered to him. "I had to go back to the room! And it's your fault."

He smiled, trying very hard not to laugh.

She sat down and saw the wine at the table. "Celebrating?"

"Yep… our new baby," and Vega was serious, and renewing our vows, amongst other things." He stopped short of saying what he was really thinking. "Ordered you a steak. Thought you might need some nourishment." Now he laughed. "Sorry, baby."

Daniel looked at his father. He hoped he grew up to be like him.

Lunch was splendid. Philip told Emma if she didn't eat some then there was no pool and he meant it. It was now past two in the afternoon. Pool time. Philip, Emma and Mikey.

Philip took Mikey on one side in the suite while Emma donned her swimsuit. Vega never let her wear a bikini, not in public.

"Don't let either one of us out of your sight. Patrick could still be here. I don't think he is, but I am not sure. Have a couple of the other guys at the pool somewhere, anywhere. What worries me is that he knows we are being followed, so therefore he knows by whom. Sounds like he is getting cold feet and whatever he is involved with he wants out."

"You think so, boss? Isn't he following instructions?" Even Mikey knew.

"He is, but he was too open in front of Emma. Talk to Mac before we leave for the pool."

Three saw them at the pool. Mikey, his boss and his wife. And two or three security guards which were plainly obvious to anyone. They were wearing jeans and T shirts where as everyone else at the private pool were in swimming attire. Vega wore black Speedos that may as well have been transparent. So might Emma's swimsuit. They were at the pool for at least two hours. Sun and water, scotch and no rocks. Emma often wondered how he stayed sober on all that scotch. She thought perhaps just practice. But she did like just being with him… and the security.

"Emma, I picked out a new car. I don't want the other one back… no matter what the cost of it."

"Another Ferrari?" Emma was hoping it wasn't.

"No. An Audi."

That sounded more sedate.

"It's an Audi Avus Quattro Concept."

"Sounds nice, Philip," she relaxed as she lay on the lounge chair next to him. "What color is it?"

"Silver, babe. Wasn't expensive really for what it does." And he was really serious.

"How much was it?" she asked as she pulled her shades down her face and looked at him, chewing on the end of the stem.

"Four million dollars… and it's got V1 tags on it already."

Emma almost chocked on the stem of her glasses. "How much?"

"Four million… I didn't get the most expensive one…"

She was speechless.

"What? I have too much money, Em. I can never spend it all. Not in my lifetime or my sons."

"Philip, I know you are rich, but not that rich just to spend that much money on a car? Are you?"

"Let's just say that the money keeps coming in… which reminds me. We need to get your money from the hotel safe. Which also reminds me. I drew up a new will couple of weeks back. If anything happens to me, Emma Vega, you will be the richest woman on the west coast and if anything happens to both of us, our children and grandchildren will be very prosperous indeed!"

And Emma's blood ran cold. She didn't want his money, only him. Now she knew that they all knew something she didn't.

Chapter 34

Emma knew her husband owned a ton of casinos and some night-clubs. She also knew that he never dabbled in drugs. He didn't agree with either doing them or distributing them, and any one of his men caught doing that took a permanent hike. But how could he have so much money? A four million dollar car?

Vega could almost sense what she was thinking.

"Came into some money from a land deal a few weeks back. I tell you most things, Emma. Those kinds of things... I don't. You have enough to deal with without worrying your pretty little head with business." He leaned across the lounge chair and kissed her lips. "All you have to do right now is look pretty for me." He knew that didn't sit well with her. She had brains when he let her use them. But right now wasn't a good time for that. Right now the less she knew the better, and he had a feeling she was putting some things together. Wedding plans she could easily deal with. Take her mind off things. That was one reason he suggested it, the other reason was he wanted to renew them with her. He would marry her ten times over if he could.

"So you like the church, baby?" He asked her.

"It's beautiful. I'm glad you found it." She knew what he was doing. "We can have the children there, right?"

"Of course. It's a family wedding. You get to pick the music, all the clothes for the children, and of course, your own. I get to pick mine," and he laughed. He really was into this and it showed. "We sound like the Von Trapp family..."

That gave Emma an idea...

Pool time went by fast. The sun was glorious unlike like last night's rain, and both the Vega's felt refreshed. Emma noted the looks from the females at the pool to her husband. And Philip noted the ones to his wife from every man at poolside. He wasn't jealous. It was him she went to bed with at night.

"Fancy a dip in the pool?" asked Emma.

"You go, baby. I'm right here and so is Mikey. I'll join you in a sec. Just a call I want to make." He proceeded to make the call on his cell, till he looked up and saw the attention his wife was acquiring from the men in the pool. Not that it was a big pool with a lot of people, but these men were power men like he was. And some of them would know who he was, too… and certainly know that he had bodyguards round him night and day. Didn't seem to stop them. He dropped the phone on his chair and walked with great precision to the pool, calling Emma's name.

"Right here, Philip," and she turned towards him.

As he reached her, she stood up in the water and she slid her arms round his waist. Emma leaned her face on his chest, a very open gesture of love towards Philip, one that shocked even him.

"Careful, Emma. My wife might see you. She might just get jealous…" and he kissed her hair. "Come on, race you to the end of the pool," and he let go of her and started to swim.

She watched him for a second. His body ripped and left her standing. Fifty he may have been, but he was putting others to shame. She took off after him, her slim body speeding through the cool water, turning heads as she went. Philip stopped at the end of the pool, water dripping down his chest, the dark hair on him in tiny curls. His Speedos clinging to him and she caught up with him and looked up into his face, water running down her hair and body.

"Now we need to get a room!"

Inside the suite, they made love, and then showered. Emma dressed in a cool white slipover dress and not much else. She sat on the bed as Philip dressed, her damp hair hanging down her back. He was dressing in jeans and a black T shirt.

"So you and Mac going out for a night on the town then, Philip?" She played with the end of her hair.

"We'll be back in a couple of hours, if that's what you're trying to find out." She amused him. He stuffed his gun down the back of his pants. "Anyway, I wouldn't dare flirt with anyone in front of Mac. He'd come right back and tell you…" and he laughed, while he touched the end of her nose and then leaned down and kissed it.

"You'd flirt with someone?" She protested.

"To get the info I want… sure." He watched her. Her lips trembled. He kept forgetting she was pregnant. "Baby, I'm just kidding," and he sat down on the fluffy quilt next to her and took her in his arms. "Why would I want anyone but you, baby." He pulled her very close like he was protecting his child, which indeed he was. Both of them.

There was a loud knock at the door.

"Six, boss. Vinnie should be outside." Mac yelled to Vega.

"Be right with you, Mac." He gently kissed her mouth and let go of her. "I'll be back, baby. Eat something and sit out with the twins. Don't stay in here for the next two hours. We are leaving about nine in the morning for home. So we all need some sleep… including us!" and he left her.

Emma always worried when Philip was gone and tonight was no exception. She sat with his sons and Mikey. They ate. They taught her how to play poker. She picked it up fast and beat them a couple of times.

They watched as she checked her wristwatch every ten minutes. One hour went by and then another, going on three. He had told her two. It was going on nine. Mikey looked a little concerned. His cell rang.

"Yeah, boss? Everything okay with you guys? You're on you way back? Okay, I'll tell her."

Emma tried to look casual as Mikey told her they had stopped to get something at a store and they were now on the way home.

They made it by nine-thirty. Paid Vinnie off, promising him duty when they returned next week and meaning it… Him and the several other soldiers Vega had hired for the day.

Mac came in first and Emma was eagerly looking for Philip, who was right behind him, complete with a couple of packages which he was trying to hide behind his back.

"Sorry it took longer than we thought. While we were out I got to test drive a car like my new one. Pretty damn hot, too…" and he looked at his wife's face. "Didn't you tell them about the new car we have, babe…"

"No, I didn't . I can't even say it, except it's an Audi something…"

"It's an Audi Avus Quattro concept…"

"Really, Dad? My God that's awesome… how much did that set you back? Three million, four?" Daniel was bursting with enthusiasm and made no secret that his father had awesome taste. "I thought maybe you had gone to get mine and Orry's birthday gifts. Maybe at the same place?"

"Maybe, I did. But your birthday isn't for two more weeks. So I guess you have to wait…"

"Awe come on, Dad, Patrick got a Ferrari…" and Daniel stopped speaking. Bad thing to say.

Orry stood up, pushing his blonde hair out of his eyes. He crossed the room to his step-mother.

"Better watch your wife, Sir. We just taught her how to play poker. She beat us three times. She might just beat you, Sir. Maybe you should keep some money to play with her."

Emma didn't understand, but Philip did. His future attorney son was the diplomat. He was trying to tell his father to include her… in all things.

Chapter 35

Emma never found out what else Philip and Mac had done that night. Never knew that he met with another family head there in Vegas. Some thing's better she didn't know. And this was one of them. He had driven the car. His friend, the Vegas Don, had one. He'd tried it out and pretty much terrified everyone in the car at the reckless speed he drove. But they survived and had had several glasses of wine and scotch before returning home. He'd picked up chocolates on the way back for Emma, which she ate with relish. They watched a little TV and then called it a night. Sleep came an hour or two later.

The jet was standing ready as they arrived at the airport, its body shining in the early morning sun. They boarded without any problems. All was well until Philip decided he wanted to fly it.

"You can't fly the plane, Philip?"

"Unfortunately, Emma, he can. He's flown it before... many times. Had a license for a long time. Why do you think our hair is turning gray?" and Mac laughed. "Boss, maybe with your pregnant wife on board better the pilot flies it, and you sit with her?"

Vega took the hint. He looked at Emma who looked extremely uncomfortable about the subject. Vega nodded in agreement and sat down by Emma.

Flight wasn't long... just time to consume couple of scotches and a light breakfast of fruit and bagels... food mainly for Emma's benefit and the scotch for Philip.

Not a bad flight as they go, but Emma was queasy and that was with a real pilot.

The limo was at the airport and collected its passengers. Emma was looking forward to seeing the children... all of them. She counted little Andrea in that.

Going down the drive to the house, somehow it looked more imposing than ever to her. She wasn't sure why, just she was glad to be home. Home... it had taken her years for it to be her home. It was the Vega house... one shrouded in mystery and ivy claiming the walls for their own hiding what they protected. She often wondered how big it really was. Ten bedrooms, twelve bathrooms, two kitchens, playrooms, the library, pool room, two lounges, the dinning room and the basement where many unsavory deeds took place. A pool, tennis courts and the biggest garage she had ever seen. A garage... that made her think. Was the new car there? She hoped not. The last few days had been tiring and mentally exhausting. She touched her face. The bruise was still very visible, but then so was her husband's. She looked towards the door where Alex stood, along with several of the security and the children, trying hard not to look over pleased their parents were home.

The limo pulled up and Philip was first out, followed only by Emma.

"Daddy..."

Pip was on him in an instant. Pip their first born and apple of Vega's eye. The twins were next, Nico and Dante, clamoring to be picked up by their mother... and last Alessandria... almost last. Andrea Pauli Vega stood watching his grandfathers... both of them. Even at five he knew who they were. A grand welcome home.

"Walk into a door, boss?" and Alex greeted Vega.

"Yep, same door Emma did... so let's forget it!"

Alex smiled. "Yes, boss. Charlie called. He is on his way over." He said it not too loudly.

Vega looked at the house. "Good to be home, Alex... very good! Any sign of life outside the ground?"

"Seemed to go with you, boss," replied Alex, making sure Emma didn't hear.

"She knows... most of it." Philip changed the subject. "We're all going back to Vegas next weekend. Going to get married again... renew the vows anyway... and before you ask, Patrick married Alexandria and he won't be living here anymore. Ask a couple of the guys to pack up his things and get them and his Ferrari shipped to Vegas. Which reminds me… what did they do with the old VI?"

"Crowley said they kept it for evidence. Someone did try to kill you. You or whomever was driving… more than likely you. They checked Patrick's car. Nail in the tire. Deliberate. Someone had to put it in somewhere. Slow leak. Timed well, though, just when he got to the house on the right night. Someone knew what they were doing."

"Keep all this between you, me and Mac till Charlie gets here. I would rather Emma didn't know. Her last pregnancy was tough. I don't want anything to upset this one." He thought about that for a minute. He was the one that was upsetting this one… him and his son. "Let's get everyone inside." As he tuned to usher his family through the doors, the main gate opened again and a loud roaring Harley screamed through it and burst with ease down the driveway.

Charlie Hill screeched to a stop just a few feet from Vega. He parked the Harley and all but jumped from the machine.

"Andrea," and Charlie put his hands on Vega's shoulders. "Good to see you, my friend. "Walked into a door, I see?"

"We already exhausted that joke, Charlie… same door as my wife. I'm not proud of it and, so help me God, it will never happen again. Subject closed. Let's get the kids and go indoors. Emma, baby, let's go inside. Get you some rest."

She readily agreed and with the two girls holding their mother's hands, trying to pull her into the house.

"Girls, go gently with your mother, and boys go *very* gently." Could he hear himself? It was almost laughable. Maybe he should remember that comment.

"Came over early, Andrea, so we could catch up. Your wife's going to rest now there is another baby on the way? Say, Andrea, maybe you should get a hobby. Take up a sport or something." Hill laughed, but genuinely meant it. "Oh, that's right. You have taken up a sport… motor racing!"

"Not so God damn loud. I had a problem explaining it was four million bucks. She doesn't know what the car is capable of doing!" Vega glanced at Emma.

Daniel joined in. "Dad's going to let us drive the car…"

"No, I am not. Not in this lifetime!" He paused. "Orry, look after Emma and the kids for a half hour. If she wants to rest, let her do it. Daniel…"

The door closed behind them as they disappeared into the study for a good hour.

Emma took herself upstairs and to their bedroom. She had missed the familiarity of it. Her things, her clothes and Toby bear, whom she had brought with her from England. Orry could bring the children into the rooms in a few moments, bypassing Anthony outside the door. She knew why they were meeting downstairs. Knew that someone's life was in danger. She was glad Patrick had gone and yet somehow she felt sorry for him. He had worked so hard to be the next Don. Was he in on it? Who else was? All over a little boy named Vega. Or was it?

Chapter 36

Crowley visited the next day way after Vega and Hill had their stories straight. Mac and Alex were constant companions to Vega… and for the most part Daniel was included. Emma busied herself with the children. Weather being warm, it gave them time to be outside before the drabness of the Californian winter set in and, hopefully, rain. They needed it.

Couple of days passed. Crowley came again. Charlie Hill was all but living there, even brought a change of clothes.

They sat in the library smoking cigars, Vega and Charlie Hill.

"Heard from Janine today."

"Yeah," commented Vega, casually laying his cigar in the ashtray while he consumed another scotch. He relaxed back in the leather chair. He glanced out of the windows and could see the family out there, his thoughts drifting. "What did she have to say?"

"Wants to stop by and visit with me. Said she's sorry we broke it off."

Now Vega took notice. "Really. She gonna stay at your place?"

"Maybe, maybe not. See how it goes." Hill wasn't sure. Depended if what they had could be rekindled.

"Do me a favor. Don't bring her by here… don't think Emma would be too keen on seeing her… especially not right now. If she wants to see little Andrea, make excuses. I know she is his grandmother, but I don't trust her around him. Keep you eyes wide open round her, Charlie. I know what she is capable of… and her father. Mac has been doing some checking. Seems Don Santori has made some recent visits to Vegas, as in very recent, like the last two days. Made a stop to see my son and the winery. Can't possibly think why... except for the obvious reasons. Sources said he went to buy the Alehandro wines at the vineyard, of which Patrick is now in charge. Could be true but I doubt it. Why would he come all the way from Florida to buy wine?"

"He wouldn't. And Janine just wouldn't happen to want to make up now either. He probably sent her to spy. You know, don't you, Andrea that she never got over you. That's why we split up. She is still in love with you."

"I'm sorry. I didn't know." Vega stood up and moved to the drinks cabinet. He poured another scotch. "I didn't mean to hurt her. I didn't mean to hurt any of them. I was different back then, before Emma." He paused. "I just want a quiet life, Charlie, with Emma and the kids. And I can't get it. Daniel will be *made* and I will teach him, but that's gonna take years before I can retire, probably four or five. We're all getting older. But we can't go backwards. Patrick can never live here."

"Andrea, you don't have to explain to me. I see what you are going through. You are sure they are all involved in this? I mean Mac is sure and Alex?"

"Afraid so. You yourself know it's JJ. How she got back here without us knowing is beyond me. She was tracked at all times. You are sure, right?"

Charlie rose up. "I am sure. Had couple of guys investigate. Seems she came in on false papers that someone here got her. I am supposing it was Santori. He must hate you an awful lot and want that child badly, but he knows he can't get him without you out of the way. Wonder if he knows Emma is pregnant again?"

"I am sure Patrick enlightened him. I can't stop thinking about the camera in the suite. It could only have been put there by Patrick. Sick son-of-a-bitch. He watched me making love to the woman he wants, and then he sells me out to Santori. That part I cannot forgive him for. Does he hate me that much or love her that much?"

"Love is a powerful thing, Andrea. You should know that. You were willing to give your life for Emma and almost did. And she for you, and I bet she would again."

Little did they know that someone was listening to every word they said. Outside the library door each thing they said could clearly be heard even if it wasn't understood.

Charlie's cell rang. He looked. "Janine. I'll take it outside."

"Don't bring her here, Charlie. I mean it… I won't be responsible for my actions."

"What scares you, Andrea? Think you might still feel the same or really that frightened she will take Donna's child?"

Philip stared at his friend. "I don't believe you said that, Charlie. Maybe you should leave." His look was brutal.

"I'm sorry, Andrea. I had to know. I like her a lot and I'm trying hard to believe her, but like you, I think she is here for your grandchild. But maybe you should confront her… face to face, out in the open, and maybe in front of Emma, so she has no fears, either. Pregnant women have fears, Andrea, and so do the husbands of them."

Vega smiled. Charlie was right. This was his house and his estate. Maybe they should find out right now what Janine really wanted.

"Good point, Charlie. Maybe we should all be straight. Go call her back. Bring her here to see the child. I'll square it with Emma. Do it. Next couple of days we'll be busy with the ceremony in Vegas…" The penny dropped. "They are going to show up at the wedding ceremony. That's why they are here, both her and her father. Just one big happy family! Don Santori, Janine, Felicia, JJ and my son."

"What?" asked Charlie. "You really think so? How would they know?"

"Santori is pulling the strings. We sent our person in; only they got too far in, and couldn't get out. Felicia or Patrick could have told them about the wedding. Santori is behind the whole thing. If his great-grandchild becomes heir, he would be able to get the whole estate and spread his drug-based operations all over the fucking place."

"It doesn't all make sense. Where does JJ come in? We know she is here? Did he finance her to get here? They never met." And then it hit him. "Oh, my god, I started it with the baby… saying that JJ was Janine's child. Oh, God, Andrea. I did it. Dear God, I am sorry."

"You didn't know, Charlie. So many kids floating round. JJ could have been her daughter and maybe in her mind she is. JJ hates me enough to go along with the idea. Both Donna and JJ look more like me than their mothers anyway. Your theory about pregnant women might be right. Time to confront the situation. If Santori filled Janine's head with the fact that JJ was the daughter…"

"My God…" and Charlie Hill realized what a mess he had caused.

"If she is here in town, get her over here for dinner. All of us be there. Let Janine see the child. I hope she'll see he doesn't look like JJ."

"What are you going to tell Emma?"

"The truth as you and I know it. I promised her the day we married I would never lie to her or cheat on her, and I have not and will not. I gave her my word."

"I'll call Janine. About seven okay with you?" Charlie speed dialed her number.

"Fine. Get this over with today and get her on her way. I'm sure she has to meet her father in Vegas. I truly hope she is not mixed up in this. She was someone I once thought I loved very much. Maybe you can make her happy, Charlie. Apparently I couldn't." And Vega turned away almost disgusted that he had made so many women unhappy and now there was only one woman that he wanted to make happy for the rest of his life. His conscience had caught up with him in more ways than one.

Chapter 37

While Charlie made the call, Vega went to search for Emma. He explained in detail what he thought was happening and why it was a good idea for Janine to visit. First to see her grandchild and, secondly, to see how he and Emma lived together, once and for all.

Amazingly enough Emma agreed. She felt inside her that she could cope with the situation better here at the house. He also told Mac and Alex. Mac didn't think it was such the great idea as the others did.

"You sure you want her here with Emma?"

"Charlie says Janine is still in love with me. 'Bout time she saw me in my real life with Emma, not in one she thinks it's about. Charlie really likes her. He would be good for her. We are both hoping that he can make her happy and that she is not tied into to this, that she is just a pawn being used by her father. Janine always felt she owed him. So dinner will be at seven. You want to bring a date?"

"What?!"

"I said you want to bring a date?" Vega was flippant, but deep down was serious.

"I heard what you said... why would I want to bring...." He was the other grandfather and Vega had just invited him to the dinner. "Yeah, I will. Don't know who, but I will find one! Casual?"

"No. Semi-formal. No jackets. Mr. Hunter, you are invited to a family dinner. Do me a favor and go tell the kitchen. Don't really care what they make, as long as it's good. Want Daniel and Orry and the kids to make an appearance, if not stay. You know all this is going right back to Santori. He needs to learn to stay in Florida on his own ground. Not steal my family." And that was a threat, and one he was going to back any which way he had to play it.

"You mean that don't you? Is that why you are letting Janine come here?" asked Mac kind of tentatively.

Vega smiled, but never said a word to Mac and just walked away calling his children to him, who ran to him like bees to honey.

"Guys, we are having company for dinner. Got to dress up and look nice." He turned to Andrea. "Your grandmother is coming to see you, little man. Grandpa Mac will be there, and so will I."

"Emma?" the little boy asked looking up at the tall man in front of him. "She'll be there, too? Won't she?" and the child looked around for his 'mother'.

"Of course, Andrea. Emma will always be here with you." Philip thought about his wife. He'd already mentioned how he wanted her to dress for dinner. Much like she had in Vegas. It would raise eyebrows at a family dinner, but it would settle Janine's interest in him once and for all.

Vega walked back towards the house like the Pied Piper. Children following him and also security. Right now he was the prime target. Emma watched him go. That was her husband. As if sensing it, he stopped and turned back for her, his arm outstretched, his hand waiting for her.

She glowed, and came forward to take the offered hand walking with them all inside her home.

They left the children at the nursery and disappeared into their bedroom. It was now four. Dinner wasn't till seven. Plenty of time till then.

In the shower Philip could just hear his cell ringing. It sat on the chair in the bathroom.

"Damn, what can be so urgent to make them call twice. Baby, can you lean out of here and see who it is. No, you, er, probably can't, can you? Not in the position we are in." Vega laughed. "They can wait."

Fifteen minutes later they stepped from the shower.

"You are going to wear me out, babe…"

"Me? I think that might be the other way round… good job you can't get double pregnant…" and Emma smiled a girlish grin. "What do we wear tonight?" Emma was walking through to the bedroom and there, on the bed, Philip had laid her clothes. "Oh, dress up night. I like it..." and Emma caught on to exactly what was going down.

Philip came rushing out of the shower. "Car's here, baby. You want to see it?" His face was aglow with joy amidst all this turmoil.

"Sure. Just let me grab on some clothes," and she threw on shorts and top and nothing else.

Philip grabbed sweat pants and together they hastened from the suite and down the stairs both with bare feet. Mac was at the door.

"Thanks for the call, Mac. Where is it?"

Mac opened the front door and there in all its glory stood the Audi...

The timing was perfect. It would be there when Charlie brought Janine to dinner.

Philip heard Emma gasp. It was more like a silver dream machine. Power on four wheels. A new V1.

"I'm not gonna race in it, babe...just drive like I normally do," which in Vega's world meant drive it at ninety.

"Right..."

"Mac. Keys..."

Mac tossed them to his boss and Vega grabbed them and opened the door.

"Sit in it, Em. Just try it. It's for both of us."

That's what scared her the most. Both of them could die in it. She did as she was asked. It was luxurious. Sleek black leather upholstery, enough dials to fly a plane and sheer opulence surrounded it. She could see the look on her husband's face. He wanted to drive it...now!

"Want to come with me, baby. Just round the block," which meant more than likely down PCH.

"Okay," she had to face it sooner or later. May as well be now.

He started the engine. There was a rushing noise to her ears. The power was obvious, just like Vega's was.

Emma was now sure what the plan was tonight. To dazzle the enemy. Great timing for the car. She was sure it would be parked in the drive when Janine got there. Smart play by her husband. But then he was a smart man.

Nice dinner. Good wines. Whole family. New car. Next to nothing clothes. Yep, smart man, and Emma settled down in the car for the ride of her life.

Vega shot up the driveway like he'd been driving this car all his life. Gates opened and out they went on the road that connected them to PCH and freedom. And behind them, with no hope of catching them, was the SUV.

Chapter 38

Emma could see the look of power on her husband's face. She watched him carefully. He was out to prove to himself he could do this both in the car and out. They positively flew down PCH and Emma did her best not to look scared. She failed.

"Sorry, baby. Fun, though, isn't it?"

"Sure is!" she smiled through gritted teeth.

He could see her hands holding onto the seat, but she never flinched. She was as tough as he wanted her to be. God how he loved her.

He turned into a side street and the car seemed to turn with him like they were one.

"Enough for one day, and we have company in an hour or so. We better go back and at least put some clothes on before we get arrested."

'*And that's not even for the speed you are driving,*' thought Emma. "Good idea, baby," she replied.

They passed the SUV on the way back, with Philip flashing his headlights at it, and zipped into the Vega estate at least ten minutes before they did. Gates opened and the car roared down the drive. Philip jumped out of the car and Daniel was there to let his step-mother out of her side. She looked a little shaken, but her brave face was on.

"Scotch, Emma?" Daniel asked her out of earshot of his father.

"Please. Now I know why he drinks. He can't feel anything." She scurried into the house realizing that her T shirt and shorts showed more than she intended and half the household was outside looking at the car... and her.

The SUV pulled in behind the brand new car and the men of the family stood there, like kids with a new toy.

Suddenly, the bedroom window opened from the main Vega suite onto the small balcony. She pushed the doors wide open.

"Philip. You might want to join me up here and leave your car for a while."

Emma gave them just enough to view downstairs. The very short skirt with slits up the side. A halter top that fitted where it touched, and the highest of heels. She turned her head slightly and her hair blew in the slight breeze.

Mac looked at her and then to his boss…

"My God, Sir… If I was you there would be no competition. I'd be gone…" and his words were left floating on the breeze as Vega took off inside the house.

"Geez… being the boss has all the perks…" Alex put in, and he couldn't take his eyes from her. "She just gets better and better…"

"Alex…!"

"Tell me you weren't thinking the same thing, Mac? Look round you at the guys…"

And Mac did. And he saw them and he wished he had a woman like that one.

Not ten minutes later did Charlie Hill and Janine show up in his black Ferrari. She could have been Mrs. Vega. She wasn't.

Mac was the first to step forward.

"Ms. Santori. How nice to see you again. Charlie…"

"Mac. Been a long time, and it's Janine." She looked straight at the car. "Andrea's?"

"Got to be Andrea's new toy. Fast cars and fast wom…" and he stopped short of saying what he was thinking. "Sorry, Janine…"

She waved her hand at him. She looked older. Much older, like time was taken its toll on her. Her hair was graying fast and her dress made her look matronly.

Charlie was about to reply when the door opened and Philip and Emma stepped out hand in hand.

"Janine, how lovely to see you." And as he clung to his wife's hand, he shook Janine's hand.

Janine Santori stared at the pair. Emma looked like she was twenty-one and Philip didn't look a day over forty. Her look went from the extraordinarily handsome man in front of her with long salted black hair, black shirt open to his waist and the tightest black jeans she had ever seen Philip wear, to the woman attached to him. She had the shortest skirt it was possible to be decent in and a top that covered where it touched. Her tan was obvious, as was the fading bruise on her face, but also the glow about her that suggested where they had just come from.

Janine didn't quite know what to say to them. Emma smiled and clung to her husband even more.

Charlie stepped in. "Nice car, Andrea. Very nice. Even better than the Ferrari." He looked at Emma. "Stunning..." the word just escaped.

"She is, Charlie. That's what being pregnant does to her." That was twisting the knife in. Janine would know how many children they already had. "Anyway, dinner is ready," and he let go of Janine's hand. "Charlie, Janine... you go inside... Mac," and he was looking for Mac's date. "Mac... your date here?"

"Here she comes now." He whispered near Philip's ear. "Best I could do on short notice. Janine doesn't know her."

"Jonas?!" Vega looked shocked and tried hard not to show it as the taxi pulled up and Mac started forward to escort her from it. "Did Charlie now about this?" his voice very low so no one else would hear.

"Yeah, I called him and asked did he mind. I couldn't reach you. You were off playing with your new toy, boss. Doesn't bother him if she's here. It doesn't bother you, Mr. Vega, does it?"

"Not me. I couldn't care less. Strange bedfellows you guys have. Glad I only have one..." and he and Emma entered through the large oak doors and back into the house.

Daniel and Orry were seated at the table and stood to welcome the guests. There were smaller children everywhere and as Charlie ushered Janine into the room she couldn't help but notice the splendor of the house. Her father's house was not this prosperous. She knew that Vega did not deal in drugs and her father did. And her father also moved in the trafficking world of young women, something Vega despised with a passion. And yet the wealth was overwhelming and so was the lifestyle.

Daniel introduced himself. Janine asked where Patrick was. That was a shock. Didn't she know he was married now?

Alex seated them all at the table. All arranged with intent and purpose. Security was high, but concealed.

Janine looked around at the children, not totally sure which one was her grandchild. And then she spotted him. A very dark-brown-haired child that looked like Andrea. Her heart missed a beat. He was gorgeous. Big brown eyes and a future lady-killer like his grandfather. Big tears welled up in Janine's eyes. At last she had met her grand-child from a daughter that she and Andrea had produced. Donna. And she knew now that JJ was not the mother as she had been led to believe. Her father had lied.

Vega saw the tears in her eyes and he stood up and moved round the oval table towards her. He took little Andrea with him.

"Janine, I would like you to meet your grandson, Andrea Pauli Vega. He is my, rather, our daughter's son, with Mac Hunter's son, Marc. Donna married Pauli Vega, my cousin the day she was killed by JJ's allies, my daughter by someone else entirely. Pauli Vega was my father's sister's child born out of wedlock, but a Vega no less. And so little Andrea is legally a Vega and will live here and your father will never get his hands on him. If he tries, it will be over my dead body. You are welcome to see him whenever you are in town with Charlie. I want only the best for you."

There was total quiet in the room. No one even blinked but it was clear now why Vega had invited her. Mac commended him. Charlie could see his point. Janine really didn't know what was going down. She put her arms out to the child and Andrea turned away running to Emma.

"Emma? The lady is not going to take me away is she? You won't let her, mommy?"

And Andrea Pauli Vega said it all.

Chapter 39

Emma lifted him onto her lap and he clung to her.

"No one is taking you away, Andrea. You will stay here with the twins and your step-sisters." It was hard to explain to a five-year-old exactly who he was.

Charlie reached his hand to Janine. She was innocent and he felt sadness for her. Jonas watched him. He had a tenderness for Janine that he hadn't had for her. And it was obvious that Janine still held a candle for Vega, who was attached to his wife for life.

With dinner pending, the children departed the room. Only Mac and Jonas, Charlie and Janine, and Vega and Emma remained. Daniel and Orry excused themselves, but promised they would be near at hand if needed. Alex stood guard duty and sampled the food as it passed by him on its way to the table.

Both scotch and wine graced the table and a fine feast of mostly Italian food filled plate after plate. Vega noticed Emma yet again hardly ate.

"Baby, you have to eat something, especially now you are pregnant. You are way too thin, baby. You need some meat on those bones." Vega slid his arm round her and pulled her to him.

Jonas spoke first. "Congratulations, Emma. That makes five, right?"

"Yes, it does. A little boy this time, I hope. I know that's what my husband wants. Right, Philip?"

"As long as it's healthy and you are, too, I don't mind which sex it is. Maybe we'll get lucky and get two again," and Vega laughed and knocked back a scotch at the same time.

"You must be very happy, Andrea, having all these children round you and such a lovely young wife to give you many more."

"I am very fortunate, Janine, that Emma came into my life. And I do hope we have more children. But I married her because the day I met her, I fell in love with her. The very first second that I saw her face. Then I found out she was married." He snuggled into her hair. "Fortunately for me, not happily. And I brought her back here. Sick, hurt from an accident, came for a vacation and she's still on one…"

"He's joking. Living here is a fulltime job. Someone has to supervise my husband. Right, Mac?" She grinned mischievously at him.

"They sure do. And you do a damn good job of keeping Don Andrea in tow." Mac was enjoying this. He was also enjoying the company of Jonas, much to his surprise. He had not expected that. They seemed to have a lot in common. Before she was always with Charlie, and Charlie seemed very content with Janine.

"Anyone want dessert?" Vega laughed. Double meaning.

"I should think about going. I have to get back home." Jonas was looking kind of sad at going and it wasn't the thing about Charlie either. It was Mac.

"Why?" Mac said it before he had thought about it. "Mr. Vega has spare rooms here."

"Well, if he wouldn't mind…" and she looked sideward at Mac. The feeling was mutual.

Vega found it amusing. "I don't mind at all." He turned to Charlie. "You want to stay, too? And Janine." Now it was thin ice. "You've been here most of the week anyway." Philip squeezed Emma's arm slightly giving her a hint.

"We can get a room made up for you, Janine. Then you can see your grandson in the morning." She was being Emma and polite.

"Let's go out by the pool. Eat desert there. Maybe another drink. Alex…" and as Vega asked for it, it was done.

The air outside was refreshing. A beautiful evening. No smog, just fresh air. Vega breathed it in… very deeply. He walked with Emma to the tables by the pool. Why wasn't it always like this? He took the best seats on the couch by the pool, Emma next to him, his hand across her legs and just under the skirt… just gently.

Alex made sure they had drinks and whatever dessert they wanted. Daniel and Orry joined them. They both had a scotch. Vega didn't mind tonight. Emma leaned on him soaking up the quiet time. No kids, just grownups. She looked at Janine. She felt sorry for her. But she really had grown away from the type of woman that Vega needed. She was much more suited to Charlie Hill. They made a great couple and she wished them well. And Mac was obviously very comfortable with Jonas. What an unlikely pair. Mac the personal bodyguard. Rough, tough, strikingly handsome. Blonde, grandfather... and Jonas. Dress that was painted floral and legs up to her neck, also long dangly earrings. Maybe it wasn't a bad match. She'd give Mac a run for his money and at least she would stop letching after Philip. Yeah, maybe they were both good matches.

Emma sipped her wine. One wine against Philip's six scotches. In fact they all drank... a lot.

Charlie glanced round the pool. There was security everywhere. He scuffed his boots on the ground by his chair.

"Expecting a war, Andrea?"

"Nope. Just preparing for battle."

Mac thought that was right. Both outside and inside the house.

Vega wanted to smoke. He couldn't round Emma.

"Baby, mind if we go smoke?"

"Not at all, Philip, as long as you don't catch fire!" Emma quipped.

"Mac... you got cigars? My wife is allowing me to smoke..." and he winked at Emma. "I thought I was on fire... me and the new car."

"You always are, baby," and Emma blushed as she paid her husband the compliment.

Charlie stood. His black pants moving with him. He looked good for a man in his sixties.

Mac, Charlie and Vega moved away from the women. It was all part of Vega's plan. Now it was up to Emma. She would talk to the ladies, especially Janine. The twins were close by if they were needed. Daniel especially was close.

"So where you planning on sleeping tonight, Mac?" and Vega laughed. "Guest room is big enough for two!"

"I just met her... well, met her without Charlie here being her date. She's quite some woman."

"Yeah, when she isn't making cracks about screwing your boss..." Charlie added.

"She didn't tonight..." Pause for thought.

"No, she didn't. I noticed that. Probably because he had his hand on his wife's legs..."

"Excuse me, guys. I am standing here." Chimed in Vega.

"We know. We also know we can't compete with you. One was your girlfriend and one wanted to be... now you have Emma, we get a shot at the ladies!" and Charlie Hill was dead serious.

And Vega wondered just how serious a comment that was.

Chapter 40

If the two ladies thought downstairs was opulent they hadn't seen upstairs yet. Emma took them on a short tour. The floor was patrolled by security, something she had learned to live with. She showed them their rooms, if they needed them and then the Vega suite.

Nothing prepared them for the inside seclusion of its splendor. Just nothing. The lounge, wet bar and small gym all refurbished to Emma's taste. Dark knotty pines graced the main room and comfy couches took stage center. The wet bar was full of anything Vega wanted and a small refrigerator was well disguised in the wall. Red velvet drapes closeted the windows in secrecy that opened to balconies on one side of the house.

They entered the bedroom, not so much a bedroom but whole suite. Emma heard Janine gasp. The bed was giant-sized... more than giant and decked in creams and beige with an odd red velvet cushion thrown on the bed, Toby bear and a fragrance filled the air. The bathroom door stood open allowing them to view the Jacuzzi of marble and showers, and wash basins with gold taps. Fluffy beige towels were everywhere, perfumes, soaps... too much to take in.

"My God... I didn't know people lived like this..." Jonas could not hold the words back. "This just for the two of you?"

"This suite is off limits to anyone. Philip only allows Mac and Alex mostly to come in here." She was doing her job well. Showing where she and Philip made love... and, as if on cue, her husband entered the suite.

"Emmy..." and he came into the bedroom and slid his arms round her waist, kissing her neck. "You showing them round?"

If ever the two women doubted Vega's love for Emma, they didn't now. Out there and in public.

"Nice estate you have here, Andrea. You have done very well for yourself… and for your family." Janine commented looking away from the pair and towards the windows. It was sinking in slowly that this was Andrea's and Emma's life. Not hers. She smiled. She really had lost him for good. But now it was okay. He was obviously very happy, and it was time she found herself a man and got on with her life. A good place to start would be with Charlie Hill.

"Thank you, Janine. I do hope that you will have a pleasant stay tonight. Charlie will show you to your room. In the morning we will all have breakfast and you can spend time getting to know your grandson."

"Thank you, Andrea. I do appreciate all you're doing." Her voice was calm.

There was an undertone there that he caught and he smiled at her and dipped his head. They walked back into the lounge.

"And, Jonas. Mac was looking for you. He is downstairs in the lounge. Emma and I are going to get some sleep. Been a long day. Right, babe?"

"It has. And a scary one." She smiled at the ladies and snuggled into her husband's arms. "I will say goodnight here and will see you both tomorrow. Philip, I'll be in the Jacuzzi," and she left them there.

He walked them to the door where Charlie stood. "Would you escort them, Charlie? I just got an invitation…" and he ushered them out and closed the suite door.

Charlie knew all too well what that was. Mac joined them on the stairs. He eyed Jonas. He would be only glad to spend the night with her, but not tonight. He and Alex need to keep an eye on their boss. He had made the point to Janine, but she was still a Santori.

Charlie found a way to occupy Janine. He took her to bed. Wasn't the first time and wouldn't be the last. Vega knew he would. He hoped Charlie would make her happy. And he hoped that Jonas would make Mac happy. They all needed someone in their lives. Especially these men.

Philip didn't sleep. He made love to his wife till almost dawn, and while she slept, he lay back on his pillows arms and hands under his head. He stared at the ceiling. The fan spun round and round making shadows as the morning light peeped through the windows.

Emma turned to him talking her sleep.

"Emmy, baby, you're talking in your sleep, babe..." and he cradled her in his arms protecting her like he always would.

She snuggled into the hair on his chest and wrapped her arms round him.

He listened to what she was saying. She was talking about their wedding... and how nervous she was. He smiled. He was looking forward to it.

His cell rang and Emma woke.

He grabbed it. Too late.

"Sorry, baby... Yeah, Mac. You can't find him? Probably with Janine. Look in the last bedroom on the left. It's nine already? I'll be down. No, I haven't slept. You?" And Vega laughed. "Thought you wanted to..." and Philip whispered into the phone turning away from Emma. "I'll be down."

He left Emma curled up in bed. She had dozed off again. He threw on some sweats and went down to breakfast in the dinning room.

They were all there before him, including Daniel and Orry and every kid he had. It looked like a playschool.

"Morning, boss? Sleep well?" asked Mac smirking.

"About as good as Charlie did! How about you?"

"I slept just great, thanks. Next time I don't plan to, though. And there will be a next time, boss." And Mac winked at Vega, a knowing look between two men.

"Bring her to the wedding at the weekend, Mac. As long as security is taken care of there. I think it would be just fine to do so. I am sure Charlie will bring Janine. At least I would know where she was and Charlie is quite capable of keeping control of her." He paused. "Say, has Emma mentioned anything to you about the wedding?"

"No, boss, not really. Why?" She had, but he couldn't tell Vega that. Emma and he had talked a lot about the upcoming renewal of vows. He had even helped her pick out the music, and was about to help her with her dress. "Where is Emma, anyway?" He had to change the subject. Mac wasn't good at lying. "Ah, there she is."

Emma all but swept into the room. Clad in the shortest shorts and a form fitting T shirt with a turned up collar, hair pulled into a pony tail, she was greeted by a half dozen kids all pulling on her to get her attention. Her daughters won.

"Good morning, everyone. My husband forgot to wake me." She glanced at Mac, who was giving her signals that he wanted to speak to her, inclining his head towards the open door to the patio "Mac, can you help me with my daughters. They want to go outside."

"Of course, Mrs. Vega."

Philip did a second take. Mrs. Vega. Mac never called her that except when it was formal business. Something was going on. He had a good idea, but he sure didn't want to spoil anything she might have planned.

Philip and Jonas watched them.

"So, beautiful house you have here, Sir. And Mac tells me next week you are renewing your vows in Vegas."

"We are. I think Mac would like to escort you, Jonas. It's formal so ask him to take you shopping, on my tab." And Philip helped himself to ham and eggs, and made up a plate for Emma. "Excuse me. I need to find my wife before these get cold."

Jonas watched him go still thinking he was sex on two legs. She looked past him to Mac. Now there was a man she could sleep with and feel good the next morning. She couldn't have Vega. He was 'very' taken and Mac Hunter sure wasn't a bad next in line.

Chapter 41

There was three days left before they returned to Vegas and much to do. Two nannies were in charge of the children and two bodyguards assigned. Vega didn't want his wife to have to worry about her children. The household became a buzz with wedding arrangements. One would think it was the first time they got married. Vega had noticed that she and Mac kept whispering about plans. He thought it was amusing and every time he asked Mac, he feigned ignorance.

Charlie let Janine stay at his house rather than a hotel, and Charlie had intervened with her father. Santori had called for her to head up to Vegas. Janine declined. She no longer trusted her own father. He had lied. When Charlie was with Vega Janine came with him. It wasn't safe for her to be on her own. Santori had long reaching fingers. Charlie's off and on relationship only grew and blossomed. Within a few days he knew he wanted to live with her. Too soon for marriage ... but not too soon for them to share his home.

Mac spent his evening off with Jonas and returned next morning. Made Vega smile. At last!

Alex was to be in charge of the wedding. Mac was to have a date. He was also father of the bride. Emma had chosen him and he was honored. Daniel and Orry were the best men. Philip did not want to choose between them. That wasn't right, so they both took the honor. New suits all round including Mac. New everything for everyone.

The children were excited. They were going to Vegas. They didn't know what that meant, but they were excited. Emma was extremely nervous. She stopped eating. This wasn't good.

"Baby, if you get any thinner, you will disappear. You that nervous?" and he reached for her in the Jacuzzi.

"A little. I didn't know what I was getting into the first time. This time I do…"

"That bad, huh?" remarked her husband.

"Not at all… I just have four children now plus one and two grown up ones. And a whole household of them. I could eat some ice cream though."

Vega picked up his cell that lay by the side of the Jacuzzi.

"Mac, bring up some ice cream. Leave it by the bathroom door. It's for *Mrs. Vega.*"

Philip closed the cell. "Eat the whole thing, babe…" as they sat down on the couch.

"Tastes great, Philip." As she licked the spoon clean and there was nothing left on the bowl except the pattern.

"You want some more, Emma? I am getting a steak sent up. You want more ice cream or some chocolate?" Any food was better than no food. "How about champagne or a glass of wine?" Got calories. He said what he was thinking. "Emma, what is bothering you? Something is." And as he pulled his robe round him, he pulled her closer to him on the couch. The windows were open and the evening breeze was still warm for this time of year.

"It's nothing…" she hesitated.

"Emma, I have not lived with you for all these years without knowing when you are lying. Now, what is it?" He turned her bodily to him so he could see into her eyes.

She looked at him. "Will we be safe in the church?"

"That's what's worrying you?" He looked at her. And maybe she was right. It was a concern to them all. That's why he had brought in so much security and also knew where Patrick and Santori were. He had spent the last few days knowing everything there was to know. The only thing he didn't know was where JJ was. Only that she was involved. Janine was now not a threat… the others were. Should he tell her the truth? She would know, like he did, that he was lying.

"It goes with the territory, babe. It's as safe as anywhere we go. I have hired extra security to be there in with the guests."

"Guests? What guests? I thought It was just family?" She looked shocked.

"It is… The Vega family." End of conversation.

She leaned back on him knowing not to push him any more than she had. That would be undermining him and he wouldn't take that even from her.

"When do we fly up there?" she asked tentatively.

"Friday afternoon. Your dress all done with?" He was being nosy.

"You mean have I got one, yes… Mac helped me pick it out."

"That's what you two were whispering about the last few days." He sipped the scotch that had patiently waited on the table to be consumed.

So he had noticed.   She would warn Mac to be on his guard.

Vega opened his cell and speed dialed.

"Mac, ask the kitchen to send up a steak, rare and more ice cream and wine for her ladyship here. Maybe some chocolate cookies, too… and Mac, thanks for helping her pick a dress."

Too late to warn him. Philip glanced sideward at her. It wasn't the dress. She was hiding something and so was Mac. But she looked happier since they chatted. Maybe she really was nervous. She sat bundled in her white robe which was much bigger than her.

"Emma, baby… you are happy, aren't you? I mean if you aren't you would tell me?"

"Oh, Philip please don't ever think that I am not. I love you so much. I would die without you. If you hadn't come into my life, I don't know where I would be. I am looking forward to the weekend so much." She leaned into him and kissed his lips, her fingers tracing lines down his face.

He couldn't resist her, nor did he want to. Eating could wait.

Mac knocked at the door. No answer. He set the tray on the table next to the door and smiled. He had a feeling that Emma had distracted Philip to take his mind off other things.

Morning came early. Friday morning that was. The whole house was in an uproar. Emma had had her chance to talk to Mac. Philip gave it to her on purpose. Suitcases stood packed, cars were ready outside to take the whole party to the plane. It was the first time the whole family had flown together.

Emma was a little overwhelmed. All this was for her.

Charlie and Janine drove up to Vegas and took Jonas with them. An odd combination for a trip. Charlie who had slept with both of them. Then again, Philip had slept with two of the three as well.

At the airport, security was tight. Vega had the feeling that sometime over the next few days Santori would make his move against the Vega family. Mac thought the same. Some things that Janine had told him supported that fact. Made it worse now she was siding with Vega.

For a whole family with kids, it was a good flight, except when they landed and Emma threw up.

"I'll try not to do that tomorrow." She was embarrassed in front of the whole family.

"Better not, babe… everyone will be watching," and Vega laughed as he helped her to the toilet.

He stood outside while she cleaned herself up.

"She okay, boss?" Mac was very concerned for her.

"She will be. Say, Mac… You look after her tomorrow. Once again Emma is your responsibility. I know it's only to the church and back to the hotel for a dinner. But things happen, Mac. I won't be with her some of that time." Vega looked worried.

"You have a bad feeling, don't you, Mr. Vega? I can tell. You think something is going to happen in Vegas."

"I do. And if I could call this thing off I would! Gut instinct." Vega was indeed worried.

"She'll be fine, boss. I don't want to die, and you once told me if anything happens to her, I am dead!"

Chapter 42

Vega nodded his head. That Mac would be...dead!

The plane landed, cars were there to take them to the hotel. Vinnie and the local chapter of his union, so to speak. This time they stayed at The Bellagio and in a very private villa. The family stayed in the hotel, close to them but not too close. Over excited kids were hard to control even for two very experienced nannies and two security guards.

Daniel and Orry joined their father and Emma for dinner, as did Mac. They waited for Charlie and his guests who arrived not much later than the Vega plane, all due to Charlie Hill's driving. Vega had booked them all rooms in the hotel. Only Alex and Mikey were to stay in the spare bedrooms in the three-bed-roomed villa with them.

Emma and Philip sat out by the private pool while they waited for their dinner guests to settle in for the weekend. The Vega suite came with a private butler and all the service they needed.

Emma leaned back on the opulent pool chair, dangling her pretty pink painted toes in the water, having removed her high heels. They sat on the marble patio along with her glass of wine.

Philip sat next to her. Dressed all in black, hair just slightly shorter, moustache and beard groomed... looking devastating and he knew it. He was bare foot, too. His Armani shoes lay on the patio. He set his scotch down on the pool table and reached his hand to Emma.

"Tomorrow is our day, baby. Yours really. Enjoy it. Make the most of it. We won't do it again for another ten years. I'll have to save up for the next one."

"This is a fantastic place, Philip. I have never been anywhere like this. I can't thank you enough…" she smiled and those big green eyes flashed at him.

"I think you can, Emmy…" and he leaned across the chair and kissed her lips.

"Er, boss…" interrupted Alex. Sorry to bother you, but your guests are here and the meal is ready." He had knocked on the glass door to the pool, but they hadn't heard him. So he opened it and had stepped out.

"Thanks, Alex. Emma, let's go… oh, shoes might be good… they go well with that strappy black dress you almost have on…" and he laughed at her, thinking tomorrow they would be married again.

They stepped inside the room. It was aglow with candles and lights. They were all   seated just waiting for the hosts. Vega took the head seat and Emma the one opposite him.

The meal was inspiring just like one would think at this hotel. Dinner was pleasant, but Philip couldn't help notice that Mac, who was sitting next to Emma, kept chatting to her rather than Jonas. And even Jonas didn't look too happy about that.

Charlie watched Philip. It was obvious he was jealous. Charlie had not a clue why. Emma was devoted to her husband.

The food was rich and the wine and scotch even richer. And it got later into the night. For the first time ever that Emma had seen, Vega was getting drunk. She knew he could hold a lot of scotch, but he was mixing drinks and she was surprised to see this especially tonight. Mac asked him to stop. The worst person that could ask him. If looks could have killed, this one would have. Vega stood up and picked the bottle and the glass up with him.

"Andrea, slow down, my friend. Those drinks don't mix…" Charlie stated, glancing at Mac.

"What are you now… my mother?" and Vega pulled away taking the scotch outside onto the patio.

Charlie followed him. There was a lot of water out there.

"Andrea, what the hell is wrong with you? You hardly spoke at dinner… to anyone, and you are getting drunk, my friend. Are you jealous of Mac and the bond she has with him?"

"Should I be?" Vega almost pouted.

"No. You should not. He is like her big brother." He paused not sure what to say. "They have something planned for you, Andrea. Do not spoil it or you will regret it for the rest of your life, my friend!"

Vega sat down in one of the pool chairs. "This wasn't a good idea, Charlie. Coming here. Patrick text me earlier. *He* knows about the wedding tomorrow. God damn it!" and Vega hurled the glass onto the rocks by the side of the pool.

"Andrea! Stop it. Your sons shouldn't see you like this and certainly your wife can't." And then he realized what Andrea had said. "Patrick? Is he going to show up? He can't, Andrea. Oh, God, he can't." There was a look in Charlie Hill's eyes.

"Really! Of course he can't."

"You want to call it all off?"

"And break her heart? Never. It's me Santori wants! You keep Janine safe, Charlie Hill, but you keep my wife even safer. He never forgave me for getting his daughter pregnant. Not ever. And now he plans his revenge against me and my family. You understand me? Do you?"

"I understand you, Don Andrea."

And they were joined by Mac and his two sons to see what exactly was going on.

"I dropped the glass. No problem. Time we all got some sleep." Philip's speech was slightly slurred, but he was hiding it well.

Alex appeared on the scene. "You want to follow your wife, Mr. Vega?" He was being as polite as he could.

"Sure," and he muttered something under his breath that no one could quite hear.

He followed Alex into the suite, with the others keeping a very respectable distance. He was the Don and one who had a temper, especially when he was drunk. Alex led him to the bedroom door and bid him goodnight.

Vega opened the door and sitting on the over size bed was Emma, just clad in the sheerest nightgown she could find. Her hair hung down and she made no secret of wanting her husband. Her fingers painted her lips and one finger slid inside her pretty pink lips.

Philip Vega closed the door behind him and shed his clothes on the floor as he crossed the room. Tonight he was not carrying. She could see his face, one of sheer determination and she could see his chest in the lamplight, ripped and his muscles flexing. He leaned down to her and kissed her lips. She could smell the alcohol on his breath, almost taste it. She could not draw back from it, as much as she disliked the taste of scotch.

He made love to his wife as if it was his last night on earth and maybe it was.

Chapter 43

Vega woke first. Emma was wrapped around him as tightly as she could be, and on her face she wore a smile. My God he was good, drunk or sober. And now it was time to brave this day. He woke her gently.

"Em, today we go to church and renew our vows. Become man and wife again... I have new rings for us. We keep the others on chains round our necks today. It's tradition in our family." He paused as she looked up into his eyes, her hair lying gently on his arm. "I am sorry for last night. It should not have happened. I was jealous and that's an ugly virtue and not one I am used to having. I did not know how to deal with it. I have never had cause to be jealous of another man my whole life... until last night."

"Philip, there is no cause now. I have never looked at any man since I met you. You know I would give my life for you. From the first moment I saw you at the wrap party, I wanted you. I thought that was a fantasy. You were way above my league. Somehow we were meant to be together and only death shall part us... and maybe not even then. I did not know what it was to love someone like I love you."

Philip shivered.

And Emma pulled the silk sheets round them both and she snuggled into him, protecting him.

There was a knock at the bedroom door.

"Boss, breakfast is on the patio when you are ready." Alex was gone as soon as he said the sentence.

"You hungry, babe?"

"I am, for a change." Her stomach was rumbling.

"The let's go eat and then we say goodbye till we get to the church. Emmy, Mac will protect you with his life, of that I know. I need to apologize to him, too. He is my friend aside from my bodyguard. There is much you don't know, Emmy..." He rose up and donned the robe that lay across the whicker chair. "You want yours, babe," and he tossed her robe onto the bed.

They wandered outside to the pool. It was cool and the bright sparkling waterfall cascaded merrily into the water.

"Is all that food for us?"

"I guess so. Enough for an army. But we do have a long day ahead of us, babe." He sat down and nibbled on a hot croissant.

Emma did the same. They looked extremely good as butter dripped from them. The orange juice was fresh squeezed and cold. Ham and eggs... too much food for two. Too much anything for two.

Philip's cell rang. It was Mac.

"Yeah. Mac. Yep, she's here. She'll take our suite and I will dress in my son's suite. No problem... and Mac, I'm sorry about last night. Just so much going on..." He stopped short of saying about Patrick hoping Charlie had told him. He would rather Emma didn't know.

"So, Mrs. Vega. You ready to become Mrs. Vega?"

"If you'll have me," she quipped.

"I think I already did last night. Several times."

"Philip..." She hit him playfully on his arm. "You should get drunk more often." And she turned to leave him.

"You liked it like that?" and he tapped her on her backside.

"I like it with you anyway you want to play," and she smiled and skipped out of the door leaving a very startled husband.

"Honest... woman never ceases to amaze me..."

Philip collected his things as he followed behind her. Slipped on some pants and after kissing her goodbye was gone to his awaiting son's suite. He passed Mac on the way.

"Look after her. She thinks she is tough, especially after last night. She's not! But I might just get drunk again..." and he laughed and carried on walking to the boy's suite.

Mac knocked on Emma's bedroom door. "You decent, Mrs. Vega?"

"Come in, Mac…" and she pulled the robe tightly round her. "You see Philip on your way here? He left with Alex. Mikey is still here with us."

"I did." Mac was carrying his suite all incased in plastic covering. Shoes in hand. "Brought them with me so I don't have to go running back. Jonas will come zip you up or whatever one does. You need help with anything?"

"No. I am good. Maybe later. Going to take a shower. You brought my dress, right?"

"I did. Has he any idea what it's like?"

"Not a clue. Hairdresser is coming in half hour. I can't do it myself. Better get showered. Make yourself at home. There is plenty of food in this villa." And she was gone to the bathroom.

Mac looked at the bed, what was left of it. Must have been a good night. He was hanging up the clothes when Emma came out of the bathroom. She reminded him of a little kid, bundled in towels and no makeup.

"Emma…" and he paused. "If ever you need help… I am here for you… from anyone." He got the point over.

"I know that, Mac. I have always known. And I know what you mean." She sat down at the vanity mirror and applied a mere trace of makeup to her face. Her eyes were a different story. She applied shades of lilac and pink and gentle pastels that heightened the green in her pretty eyes.

There was another knock on the suite door. Mac brought in the hairdresser, who was ushered through to the bedroom. Mac stayed in the lounge. This was girl time. He changed into his suit. It was perfect. All that blonde hair and the jet black formal tux complete with waistcoat and bow tie. Vega had picked them all to perfection. He was dressed ready.

He knocked on the bedroom door. "You need any help getting into that dress, Emma. I can get Jonas…"

"Mac, you can help… the zipper is stuck…" she yelled out to him.

Mac wasn't so sure it should be him. His boss wasn't too happy with him still and now he would be in his wife's bedroom helping her dress?

"You sure? Boss already thinks we are having some illicit affair…"

"Mac, if it was going to be anyone it would be you, but I think I convinced him last night he was very mistaken…" she was laughing on the other side of the door. "Come in, Mac."

He turned the door handle and entered. In front of him was the most beautiful sight he would ever see. Her dress was amazing on her. He started at the top. Her hair was pulled tightly on her head with sprays of fresh flowers and pearls woven into her hair. Lace just hinted on the top of the pearls. Round her neck was almost a choker collar. Then a diamond shape cut-out back and front showed a lot of skin, tight to her waist and then sheer to the floor. No sleeves, just lace. Cream lace and very pale pink satin. She turned slightly and he could see the slit up the right leg that led straight up her thigh almost to her underwear with a garter underneath, peeping out on her leg as she moved.

"Your husband really is going to kill me. I let you pick this one… in a Catholic church… Oh, God… even though you look fantastic. Pure dream, lady. Pure dream."

"Help me zip the back. It's stuck at the top. Hope I don't have to breathe much… oh, and thank you…" She glowed.

And then they were ready. She carried a single rose in her hand. Mac checked that Vega had already left for the church. Now Emma was Mac's charge.

"You wearing what I told you to… adapted as it is." Big brother was back.

"I am. Why do you think the zip was stuck?" and she slipped into the pale pink high heels and they were gone.

Chapter 44

By the time they got to the car, folks were staring at Emma. She looked like a movie star. A shy one. Mac was proud to escort her and made no secret of it. They did, indeed, make a dashing pair. Jonas had come out of the hotel with Mikey and they watched. Jonas was jealous, really jealous. She could never look like that...and her new boyfriend...he certainly looked happy enough with Emma on his arm.

The car's engines purred in the noonday sun. Vinnie held the door for Emma and she slid into the seat and looked up at Mac, who winked at her. He was very proud of Emma.

Ten minutes in Saturday traffic and they were there. Mac's cell beeped.

"Yeah, Alex. Boss in there and the twins? Great. Yep, we are here. It's packed, really? Any sign of anyone that should not be here? Good. We are just getting out of the car now. See you inside. Has he any clue what she is going to do? Even better." And Mac hung up the call.

"Alex knows?" asked Emma, a little surprised.

"Had to tell him. The Twins don't know. You are going to shock your husband to death. Ready?"

"Yes..."

Vinnie held the door as Emma climbed out. He offered her a very admiring glance. Mac took her hand and they both looked up at the very old church steeped in tradition.

"Yep, he's going to kill me..."

Emma laughed and looked towards the steps. There were onlookers, couple of photographers, and faces she had no clue who they were. Mac knew. They were Vinnie's 'friends'.

Mac led her up the steps to the big wooden doors. The two nannies were there, complete with five little children all dressed up. Pink for the girls and white shirts and black pants for the boys. Janine stood there with them, ready and willing to offer help. Charlie, too...

Emma stared at Charlie Hill. He was wearing a tux just like Mac was, his long hair pulled back in a ponytail.

"My, Charlie Hill. You look dashing. Someone should up and marry you, both you and Mr. Hunter here." And she happened to glance up the seemingly very long aisle and she saw him.

Philip Andrea Vega stood out just slightly into the aisle. He was devastatingly handsome. The double-breasted tux fit like a glove and his hair shone in the lights from the ever gleaming windows. Complete with high-necked shirt, waistcoat and tie, he wore a single pink rose in his buttonhole... one that mirrored hers. Emma couldn't take her eyes off him. He looked like James Bond. A playboy with a license to kill.

Mac was amused. "Yeah, and he thought we were having an affair. Right! I wish."

Alex raised his eyebrows, but he stepped in anyway. "Everything is ready. Security is tight. Boss looks terrified... Mac, look at her face..."

And Mac did. Emma was mesmerized. All this for her and because Vega loved her so much. Tears rolled down her face and landed on her pretty pink lips.

Janine stepped forward. "Emma, I am glad he found you. He is marrying you twice. A Don who loves a woman that much is a real Don. Make him proud, Emma Vega." And with her fingers wiped the tears from Emma's cheeks.

Everyone was round her. Her Family.

It was then the music started. She watched as Philip moved further into the aisle, the twins next to him, Daniel then Orry. They were men. She could see Father Murphy in his Sunday-best attire.

"You ready, Emma?" asked Mac, as Janine and Jonas led the children up the aisle.

"I'm ready..."

From the strains of the organ came the processional song from Emma's favorite film. 'The Sound of Music' rang out as she and Mac started their journey. Heads turned everywhere watching her, while Emma was watching Vega. They walked slowly and she could hear the music, but all she saw was Don Andrea Vega standing there waiting for her to reach him.

Mac felt her hand clench tighter on his arm and he smiled. They went slowly up the aisle, the dress not allowing anything else. They neared him, just a few yards away. She looked into his face and he into hers. Never was there a more perfect couple.

Vega stepped out to greet her, and Emma let go of Mac's arm. Instead of taking her husband's arm she dropped down to the glorious red velvet carpet, bowing to his position in life. She dipped her head in supreme recognition of him and his lifestyle and she heard him gasp. So this was the surprise. It meant the whole world to him. In return, he bowed his head to her and then to Mac. And Mac smiled like 'I told you, boss'.

Emma didn't move. It was now up to Vega. He stretched his arm and hand to her and whispered her name.

"Emma." His smile to her was worth a thousand words and he winked at her, mouthing 'I love you'. She accepted his hand and stood up and together they stepped up the remaining stairs to the priest and once more become husband and wife.

He looked at her and marveled the way she had acknowledged him in public. So that was what she and Mac were talking about for days. He had been teaching her the ways of the family just for today. He wondered who else knew what she intended. She had done this just for him.

His one regret was that Pauli and Donna were not there to share this day with them. His cousin and his own daughter. And another daughter out there somewhere with an intent to kill.

Philip could feel her shaking as they reached the top of the steps to be blessed by Father Murphy. Vega let go of her hand and slid his arm round her waist. He whispered to her so only she would hear. "Nice dress, Emma. Very nice."

"Trust Andrea," murmured Charlie as he watched his friend's gesture to his wife.

And tears rolled down Janine's face.

"You, okay?" Charlie asked, most concerned.

"More than okay. They are happy together and now I can get on with my life, Charlie Hill… hopefully with you in it."

And Charlie Hill stroked his whiskers and plumped up like a peacock. Maybe she could. And, just maybe, in the next few weeks he would ask her to marry him.

Mac stood at the side watching his boss. He was a lucky man. He glanced sideward to where Jonas sat and he winked at her while she blushed.

Maybe today was a good day for them all and just maybe Vega's thoughts and fears were wrong… Mac hoped… but Vega had never been wrong in his life.

And today would be no exception.

Chapter 45

Strains of music from the twenty-year-old organ blasted through the church as Emma and Philip walked back down the aisle. They held hands like two kids and were laughing as they walked back down with all the children, and young Andrea, closest to them. Philip acknowledged the looks from his friends that were there and their families. Emma could not place them all. Some she had never seen before. But Alex had been right. It was packed with people, even if it wasn't a huge church. All filled with happy faces and some older looking Vegas gentleman that Vega would introduce her to later at dinner. They were stopped near the door by photographers snapping for professional and monetary gain.

Mac, Alex and Charlie were out there first. Mikey stayed with Vega. Both Mac and Alex had guns ready on their hips. Charlie had his just inside his jacket.

Janine and Jonas held the children back just inside the church. Daniel and Orry stepped out from behind their father. Daniel closest to him.

Philip escorted Emma down the church steps, his eyes darting everywhere, and then he saw the flash. It was binoculars glinting in the sunlight.

"Mac... to the right! By that little house." Philip yelled to him. "Get Emma into the car!"

"Philip, what's happening..." and she had no time to finish the sentence.

Mac grabbed her hand. "Let's go, Emma..." and forced her towards the car "Boss... Patrick..."

Vega turned and there, stepping from the side of the church, was his son.

"What the hell are you doing here?" and Vega looked around like he was expecting someone else to join them.

Patrick came closer and Vega could see someone had beaten him up. His eye was black and blue, and as he looked at his arm, blood dripped down through his sleeve and onto the concrete.

"I did what you said, Dad. What you and Charlie told me to do. I tried to make you proud..." and Patrick fell forward right into his father's arms. "Santori did it. And JJ. They have Alexandria." And Patrick passed out and lay there his blood dripping onto Philip.

"Alex, get the fuck over here, now." Philip was yelling as loud as he could and at the same time cradling his son.

"Mac, what is happening? What's wrong with Patrick?" She was starting to panic.

"Emma, get in the car. Just do it, please. Get in the car..."

"Not without Philip... Mac..." she screamed.

And as she said it she could see Philip standing up, blood on his tux, pulling Patrick with him, trying to support him, and almost lifting him up in his arms.

Vega was surrounded by his security, Alex at the helm, guns drawn, and waiting for trouble. Two of the soldiers took Patrick from his father. They carried him between them.

He was still out cold. Vega leaned over him feeling for a pulse. It was barely there.

"Take one of the cars. Get him to the nearest hospital." He was safe now. They had done with him. Now it was his life and his wife's that were at stake and his other son. Daniel.

Emma tried to get out of the car.

"Emma, stop it! You cannot go to him. Let them deal with this." He held her by her arms.

"You going to tell me what to do, Mac? I'm the Don's wife remember? Above your rank and file..." Emma said it knowing it would hurt him to the quick and that's what she intended, to throw him off guard and get away from him.

Mac let go of her... instantly, a look on his face she would never forget like she had stabbed him, but it gave her the space she needed and she was gone out of the car toward her husband.

"Emma, no. Go back," screamed Daniel, running after her. "Dad... ..."

It was the chance the gunman needed... the lone gun. They had been taught well by Santori. A woman was not as suspect as a man, especially not one who had come from a convent, and one who hated their father more than living itself and one who had teamed with Janine's father to be rid of her own.

All dressed in black, she stepped out from the shadows of the fugitive house, a gun in her hand. She didn't have to come closer. She could kill from there. She was busy setting her sights on her father, even through the ring of soldiers he had. And then she saw Emma. And she altered her target.

Vega saw his daughter at the same time. He burst through his own ranks and, without hesitation, ran towards Emma at breakneck speed throwing himself in between her and JJ. As he dived forward to save her, the bullet hit him square in the back. He went face down at her feet. Time stood still.

Emma saw it all in slow motion. Saw Philip fall, out cold lying on the ground. She looked up and saw JJ still with the gun in her hand. All she could remember after was what they told her. Emma pulled the skirt of her dress to one side. In the garter, tucked on the inside of her leg, she carried a gun, not just any gun, but the one Philip had given her. She pulled it clear, stretched her arms out and aimed. She squeezed the trigger and she heard the bullet leave the chamber, almost like she saw it in flight. It hit JJ in her shoulder and she dropped the gun groaning in sheer agony, her look of triumph gone, and from her other side Charlie Hill also spent a bullet. JJ died where she stood. She was no good to Santori now.

From the black limo parked across the street, Don Santori stepped out, soldiers in tow, Alexandria in their clutches and Felicia at his side. Santori had a pistol to Patrick's wife's head.

"Very good, Mrs. Vega, and please drop the gun. Perhaps you should be the Don and not your husband. He lets emotions get in the way. But I am forgetting he is now dead at your feet. Died saving you. And his son probably also dead. We did a good job on him and we have Alexandria here for posterity. Vega's men will not shoot me with her here. I came for the child. The one my daughter's daughter named after your husband. Donna was my granddaughter and Andrea is my great grandchild. He will be raised with us, a Santori. Vega lost out all round. Your husband got my daughter pregnant and I took the baby away. All those years he never knew. And now I'll have this baby." He was looking around for the children. "Janine, come outside. Your father is here. Bring the child with you. Come home with us and I will let Alexandria go."

Felicia had been listening. Santori wasn't about to let her sister go, and Santori's plan of using JJ had gotten her beloved Philip Vega killed. That was not the plan.

"Janine, come out here. Your ex-lover is dead. Bring the child."

Janine froze. Andrea was dead? Now she hated her father even more. He had lied to her about Donna and now Philip was dead.

Charlie Hill could not let Janine come out of the church. He knew that her own father would kill her. He had no regard for anyone's life, let alone anyone that had loved Vega… and Janine had. He slipped around back of the cars, virtually unseen, except by Mac, who knew now why Emma had done what she had. And Philip Vega, his boss, could have paid for loving her with his life. She really was the only woman he had ever really loved.

Chapter 46

When Emma dropped the gun, only one person noticed where it fell. She stood motionless now, afraid to move, afraid to look down for fearing if she did it would be real... and her beloved husband would be dead. Somehow she found the strength to speak.

"Let Alexandria go. Take me instead. She has Patrick. I have nothing." Emma was dead inside of her.

"Emma, no!" yelled Mac. His feelings apparent. Santori would kill her as soon as she got near him. He could see Charlie; he was almost behind Santori's car. He had to buy a little more time. "Emma, turn around and walk to me. Don't look down, Emma. Don Andrea wouldn't want that. Emma, you hear me? Turn around, 'baby'..."

She was so shocked at Mac calling her 'baby' that she turned his way.

"That's it, 'baby'. Come to me." He figured she was in shock. He was right. He put his arms out to her and slowly she moved towards him.

When she got to Mac, she collapsed in his arms. He picked her up like she weighed nothing and looked towards Santori.

"She's pregnant, you bastard... at least let her keep his child." And Mac slid her inside the car and whispered to Vinnie.

It was enough time. Charlie was behind Santori.

"*Mr.* Santori."

And Santori whirled around with the gun still to Alexandria's head.

"You have the gun to the wrong girl, don't you? It's Felicia that's in love with Mr. Vega. Oh," and Charlie paused. "While I'm here, I want to marry your daughter!"

185

Don Santori was speechless.

Charlie waited a moment.

"By the way, Santori. Little Andrea's other grandfather is very much alive. It's the gentleman with the blonde hair there. The one with his gun aimed right at you." Charlie was enjoying this. "And you might like to know that Patrick is still alive and what you tried to beat out of him, he didn't even know! None of us did till a few days ago. There was only one man that did till the other day. But I think that should come from him… right before you die!" and Charlie had Santori in his sights. He was ready and waiting.

As he spoke, the big wooden doors opened and Janine Santori stepped outside. The door closed behind her. She was a solitary figure standing there. The guests stayed inside.

"Go back, Janine," yelled Mac. "He will kill you! And anyone who is connected to Mr. Vega."

But she kept on coming. She could see Andrea on the ground and she walked towards him, terrified what she might find. Charlie watched her near her ex-lover.

"I never knew my own daughter, father… you made sure of that. I had a daughter all those years with Andrea. Someone I really loved. I'll be damned that you will take my grandchild from me. He's a Vega through and through. By birth and destiny and he will stay with this family. You cannot kill us all here. Andrea has two more sons than can take over and four more children. Are you going to shoot innocent children now? I knew what you were. A dispenser of drugs and dealing in prostitution. I looked the other way because you were my father. But now you take the life of a man I have always loved and will always have a place for in my heart. And you will not do anymore damage to this family." Janine bent down to retrieve the gun from the ground.

"Janine, no…" Mac tried to warn her.

As she leaned towards the gun, she could see Vega's hand move. She gasped. How could that be?

"Janine… move away from Don Andrea. Do it, now… *you* cannot help him." He was giving her a hint.

She understood Mac. She couldn't help him and, maybe, he didn't need the help.

Mac moved slowly towards her and his boss, never taking his eyes off Santori. Slowly, Don Andrea Vega came round. He moved his arm. Pain shot through it. But he knew he had to move. It was now or never. Mac was right by him. Almost in front of him now, and Alex had moved next to him. Janine had moved towards Mikey and out of range. To safety. The pain in his back was severe, but at least the bullet proof vest he wore had stopped him from being dead. Slowly, he rose up from the ground and grabbed Mac's arm.

"Boss…" and Mac slid his arm round Vega's waist, supporting him. Santori stared in disbelief. Vega was not dead.

"Let Alexandria go, you bastard. She is not part of this," Vega growled.

"She married a Vega. That makes her part of it… and you, I saw you shot in the back."

"You did. That the only way you ever have people shot? Not face to face. You want to try it that way. Facing me?" yelled Vega.

"Boss, no. You don't have enough strength. Let me do it…"

"Mac, no. This is between Santori and me. It always has been. But first he should know the truth." Vega paused, seeing Charlie. "Charlie, keep your gun on Felicia. If Santori kills Alexandria, make sure her sister goes with her."

"Yes, Don Andrea." Charlie knew what Vega was doing.

"Boss, I can hear sirens in the distance. They have to be coming here. Even for Vegas, three shots are too many!"

Vega leaned on Mac for support. He grimaced, Emma's gun hanging form his other hand.

"Is it bad, boss? The pain…"

"Turn around, Mac and I'll shoot you in the back, see how you feel. Hurts like hell… A few more cracked ribs, bruised shoulders… but I am alive, thanks to you and your idea." Still he leaned on Mac sliding his arm round Mac's shoulder.

"You can't even stand, boss. How the hell you gonna face him. This isn't Dodge City."

"No, it's not. But I aim to kill him, Mac. All I need is one hand. They tried to kill my son and my wife. And the Vega family settles its own problems."

Philip straightened up just a little more. Alex to his other side. Vega glanced at the car making sure that Emma was safe.

"She's fine, boss. I looked after her," stated Mac, not looking Vega's way.

"I heard you…" he said quietly. "Santori, let Alexandria go, now, or I will shoot you where you stand. Face me man to man." And Vega let go of Mac, his hand at his side. "Oh, and as the others now know, Andrea Pauli Vega is legally just that. The Pauli you knew was my cousin, Pauli Vega. Father's sister's boy. Pauli married your granddaughter the day Rossi killed them. In every way the little boy is a Vega."

Santori was red-faced and angry… his gun leveled. Vega saw him squeeze the trigger and Andrea Vega raised his gun and fired. He hit Santori dead in the heart. Alexandria fell more out of fright than anything else, but she was alive. Felicia turned to flee.

"Not so fast, young lady. I think the police would like to talk with you. With good behavior you might be out in a year or three. Maybe…" Charlie had his gun on her.

"I don't want to go to jail," she screamed at Charlie. "Andrea, please help me. Don't let them take me. You loved me once. Please, Andrea," she was begging him and as she did she grabbed her sister's arm. At the same time Felicia grabbed for Santori's gun, turning it on Alexandria, and Vega saw her. He didn't even hesitate, and pulled the trigger yet again dropping his ex-lover where she stood.

"Wrong, Felicia. I never loved you!"

Charlie stared at Vega. He was indeed a stone cold killer.

And now it was over. Santori and Felicia lay dead. His soldiers scattered leaving them where they fell. Janine stood motionless till Charlie Hill walked to her.

"I'm sorry, Janine. Andrea had no choice."

"I know he didn't. I knew it would end this way. Did you mean what you said Charlie Hill… do you want to marry me?" her face expectant.

"I do. I think, though, there is one man we should get permission from. He is standing over there, and how he is still standing, I have no idea."

Chapter 47

Vega dropped the gun. It was done. He leaned slightly to the left. Mac caught him as he fell, hurt far worse than anyone knew.

"Alex, help me with him!" and Mac caught him before Vega hit the floor.

Alex was there in a flash while Mac cradled his boss in his arms.

"Get Mikey. Help me get Mr. Vega into the car. Need to get him back to the hotel. He's out cold. He knew it would end this way." All the sentences came out in spurts. "Tell Daniel and Orry to look after Emma, and take a couple of soldiers with them. We need them back inside the hotel all in once piece. Let's go. Charlie, will you explain to the police? Tell them anything, self defense, anything. They can talk to the boss later. Delay the dinner. Everyone in the church knows the situation. Either that or just send them home. Your call, Charlie!"

They lifted him bodily into a separate car. Wasn't the trip back that had been planned or the night that Vega had had in mind for he and his wife. He had arranged for champagne, flowers, chocolates and more to be in the villa. Couple of luxurious gifts for her and certainly a night with him she wouldn't forget. She was getting that alright!

Both cars arrived back together. The less the hotel knew the better. It wasn't their problem. The dinner planned was.

The twins escorted their step-mother in another car. She didn't even remember the ride home, nor arriving at the villa. She was in shock and it showed. Daniel took her hand and led her into the lounge. She sat on the couch not knowing exactly what was going on.

"Philip…is he…" she couldn't finish the sentence, her big green eyes full of tears.

"No, Emma. He just out of it a little. He was wearing a vest. All the men in the wedding party were…including us."

"Can you unzip my dress…I can't breathe, Daniel…" and Emma was struggling to pull it from her neck, but the zip was stuck.

Daniel moved to the back of the couch and unzipped the top. Lo and behold she was wearing a vest also. "You, too? Mac's idea, I bet."

"Yes. He thought it might be me they shot and …" she stopped. "Philip, where is he? You said he…"

"Dad's okay. He was shot in the back. He passed out after killing Santori and Felicia." Daniel shook his head. It was obvious Emma knew nothing about what happened and that was probably for the best. He doubted she even remembered shooting JJ and probably they should keep it that way. "Mac and Alex are bringing him back. It's over Emma. Santori is no more, nor is JJ. Felicia had it coming, too. But it's over."

As Daniel spoke, the villa door opened and they helped a very out of it Vega into the bedroom, one man supporting him under each arm. It had taken Vega five minutes to end it all.

Emma jumped up and followed them, the boys with her. Gone were her shoes and hanging half-undone from her neck was her dress. The twins had discarded jackets and vests, leaving behind a pile of clothes on the couch.

Emma all but fell into the bedroom and towards the bed.

Mac caught her. "Emma…let us look after him. Remember, like last time. You wait here with Daniel. He's going to be fine. Bullet is in the vest, not in him. He's bruised and more than likely has more cracked ribs. But he's fine…need to get his clothes off him. See the damage."

And she watched as Mikey and Alex took his bullet proof vest off. There was just a tiny trickle of blood running down his arm where the bullet had pierced the vest. He was lying face down and vast bruising could be seen on his back. If it had not been for the vest he would surely have been dead. More than likely that's why he was out cold now. She watched as Mac put pressure on her husband's back, felt his ribs and turned him slightly to look for further damage.

She put her hands out to Daniel and Orry. These were his sons. This wasn't just about her. She felt Orry tighten his grip on hers and Daniel let go of her hand and put his arm round her. This was her family and she thought of her children.

"Daniel, where are my children..."

"Janine and Jonas have them. They are safe. So is little Andrea."

She quieted then. "Can I get my robe?"

Mac handed it to her from the bed. "Emma turn round," and he unzipped the whole dress for her.

She clutched the front of the dress, took the robe and scurried to the bathroom to change and let her hair down from the flowers and pearls. She was gone longer than needed. Mac went after her. He knocked on the door and didn't wait.

She was staring in the mirror like she didn't believe things were happening round her, dress still clutched to her chest. She had removed the vest, and had slid her arms back into her gown. She heard Mac behind her.

"I could have got him killed, Mac. Couldn't I?"

"But you didn't, Emma. He's just fine." He looked at her as she turned around to face him still in her fancy dress. "Hey, come on. It's okay," and Mac pulled his boss's wife to his chest and held her there, his hands on her back.

Emma cried uncontrollably. "I shot someone, didn't I?"

"Emma, Emma...you had no choice. You were defending your husband. You didn't kill anyone. Charlie did. It's okay to cry," and he held her tightly while her cries escalated.

And Mac knew now there was no future with Jonas. He had not known till now how much he cared for Vega's wife. When he had called her 'baby' it brought it home to him. Wherever they went he would be there for her, in silence. She would never know and most certainly Vega would never find out, for if he ever showed it... he was 'a dead man walking'.

Chapter 48

In the other room Vega came out of his slump. His back hurt like hell and he turned his face towards the bathroom.

His voice was weak. "Emma," and he called for his wife.

She ran from the bathroom leaving Mac thinking that he must have been insane to hold her in his arms. He vowed to himself it would never happen again. It couldn't. He and his boss had a grandchild between them, one that Vega would protect till his dying day... and he and Vega were friends.

She dropped down on the floor next to the bed and leaned over the side to him. Alex and Mikey stood back while she talked to him, their conversation all but a whisper. Philip tried to rise up into a sitting position. Alex was immediately there to help him.

In the bathroom, Mac was trying to compose himself. He looked through the mirror. Enough. He walked out into the bedroom. Vega didn't seem to notice where he came from.

"Mac, where is everyone from the church? You can still hold the dinner... go ahead. Bride can go down with you."

"Without the groom?" Mac asked his boss, looking at Alex as he said it. But obviously Vega was suspicious.

"I can make it down there for a little while. Alex and Mikey will help me. Charlie's still here, right? Jonas and Janine? How did she take to me topping her father?"

"She understood. Charlie is with her and the kids... and Jonas." Mac added.

"Your date, right?" and Vega looked at Mac and gave him the strangest sideward look. Maybe he better keep seeing Jonas a while longer.

"They are all here. Patrick is comfortable at the hospital. He was awake almost straight away. Says he has things to say to you…"

"I bet he does… including how much he loves my wife…" doubled-edged statement from Philip Vega.

Vega knew. Mac cringed. Why the hell had he called her baby out there in front of everyone? It was the only way he could get her to come to him. It had worked and not because Emma felt anything more than friendship for Mac… her big brother, her father figure.

"I don't want to go without you, Philip. I'll wait. I still have on the dress and I can do something with my hair… I just need to do it back up…"

She didn't get to finish. Vega slid his hand into her hair and she turned her face into his palm and he caressed her cheek. "I'll come with you, baby. Alex, help me up. Mac…"

They raised him up from the bed and he sat on the end of it still sporting his jet black pants. "I need something to wear. 'Baby', get me a shirt to wear. Something nice. My tux jacket is ruined."

Emma left him for the closet and picked out a black shirt with high collar, and no need for a tie. But Mac heard the 'baby' very clearly. Vega was more than making his point.

She handed him the shirt and Alex helped him put it on. He flinched as the shirt touched the savage bruising on his back. The slight bleeding had stopped and a small bandage covered the tiny hole. He buttoned it up and then, with a little help, stood up.

"You want to tidy your hair, Em? Here," and he twisted it into a twirl on top of her head and pushed a pin into it. It stayed. "Not bad. Maybe I'll give up my day job," and he laughed, choking just slightly. "Maybe I won't laugh. Let's make an appearance at least. Put everyone's mind to rest that we are still alive." He paused. "What happened to JJ? Did they take her and Santori away?"

"Charlie said they did. Police took them. No one from this side was arrested."

"Who shot JJ?" Vega really didn't know for sure.

Mac went to answer him.

"I did, Philip." Emma owned up to what she had done. "I shot her when she shot you. I'm sorry, but she shot you and I thought you were dead." She couldn't look her husband in the eyes.

Vega pulled her to him and cradled her as best he could, as far as his bruised back would let him. "It's ok, baby. You did what you had to do." He kissed her hair.

"Charlie finished it off…" continued Mac quietly.

"Good," was all Vega said.

"Boss, you really think you should go to dinner?" asked Alex very politely.

"I do. Just to show them I am alive if nothing else. Where is Charlie now?"

"With your children and the ladies. He dealt with the police for you. They won't bother you, boss," Mac replied casually. "You need help to the dining room?"

"I'll be fine. You and Alex be right behind me. Mikey, watch the twins."

"Boss," interrupted Mac. "Patrick said something about you and Charlie… did you plant him in with Santori? Was he on our side all the time?"

Vega paused. He looked round the room. They were all expecting him to say something profound. "Patrick crossed the line. He made a pass at my wife. He was only supposed to make it look like that, not follow through on it, so that Mac and anyone that saw him were convinced. Everyone had to believe his actions were for real. But no one makes a pass at my wife… no one," and Vega looked straight at Mac. "Patrick was a plant. Only Charlie knew. The whole time he was working for me, but he will not be the next Don. To be honest, tonight, I thought he was dead. He's my son. Santori must have found out somehow that he was still working for us…not sure how. Patrick changed the last two years. He is not the man he was, and maybe that was my fault. I pushed him. He will be better at the winery, a married man, with his own destiny, but I need to talk to him tomorrow. I want him to know he did do well. But it was a scam. Everything you all saw was. Once or twice Charlie and I nearly slipped up, but we had to get Santori here to us and he came. We knew he wanted Andrea a few months back. He let it slip in front of Felicia. She came to me. I couldn't tell anyone, especially not you, Emma." He looked at his wife. "You would have thought the worst...and no, nothing happened, baby. I turned her away." He stretched his hand to Emma, who took it gladly.

He continued. "We also knew he couldn't take the child away. It was either get him to come after the child or me to use my old charm... well, Janine was a long time ago and I am a very happily married man. Two choices only. So Patrick volunteered to side with them against me. Kinda in contempt of me and using Emma as his reason for leaving. Santori brought JJ home. She was eager to kill me and almost succeeded. She had to be the one to cut the brakes. That's who Mac saw with binoculars. Felicia, well at that point, she was just along for the ride. Vengeance. Apparently she was also sleeping with Santori. Always was a wh... well, never mind." He knew if he said whore, that it made him one, too.

Emma realized that Philip was speaking thoughts out loud tying up loose ends.

"Philip, may I come with you to the hospital..." she asked, looking up into his face.

There was total silence in the room. Daniel watched his father very carefully. This was a learning process for him. How to be cunning and clever like his father. The twins had been quiet all the way through this.

"Why?" Vega asked her.

"Because I am your wife."

"Good enough answer! You may," and Philip was proud again of Emma. "Today, yet again, I lost a daughter. But Mac and I gained a permanent grandchild, and Daniel your future is safe now. In two weeks you will be 'made' and I will teach what you need to know. You will be the next Don Andrea Vega."

Chapter 49

Next day, Vega, Emma, Mac and Charlie Hill visited Patrick. Mac wondered which one looked worse, his boss or Patrick. He thought Vega. Why didn't Patrick look worse? And then it clicked. Santori wasn't the ring leader, Patrick Vega was. Patrick's beating was a disguise. That's why they didn't kill him. They couldn't... and Patrick had used Alexandria, too. No wonder she had returned home distraught.

How did Mac know this... because he loved Vega's wife, too. That's how he knew. Did Vega know? That was the point, and if so, what was he going to do about it... and him.

The hospital visit wasn't long. Neither was the trip back to the hotel. Vega waited till everyone was seated in the villa including his wife. It included Mac, Mikey, Alex, Charlie and the twins.

Vega looked to the window out onto the pool. It was peaceful and tranquility was outside... not in this room. He stretched his back. It hurt, so did his heart. He knew what had to be done. Neither he nor his wife would be safe as long as one of the 'Family' was still alive. But this one he could not do himself. He needed a volunteer, and it had to be done before they left Vegas. He walked to the bar and poured himself a scotch.

"Boss, I could have got that for you..."

"You could, Mac... but you didn't..." Vega looked down at the drink and rolled the glass in his fingers. He pursed his lips. This was tough even for him. "Mac, I know you are in love with Emma... so please spare me the explanation you are not. Oh, maybe not like my son is, but you are none-the-less. You gave yourself away yesterday outside the church. I had my suspicions for a long time." Vega stopped. He looked straight at Mac, who wasn't even red-faced and looked his boss back in the eyes. And then he looked at Emma. She looked horrified. She had no clue, and he had put her in the shower the night her husband hit her.

"Oh, my God, Philip. What are you saying? That can't be right? Mac is like my father!" Emma was not happy about this.

"In your eyes, baby. To you, yes." Philip watched her. She really had no clue about this. Vega heard Charlie and Alex gasp. They had no clue either. Mikey didn't look surprised. Then nothing fazed Mikey. Daniel looked like he wanted to kill Mac. He had broken his father's trust. And Philip looked back at Mac.

"I have never betrayed you, Don Andrea, and I never would. I have never touched your wife, and have no intention of doing so. I am totally loyal to you." He looked Vega straight in the face.

"I know you are, Mac. Of that I have no doubt. I wanted it in the open. How it will affect us all… remains to be seen. I think that when Daniel takes my place, you will stay in California with him. We shall see. But Mac is not the priority right now. My son is."

Daniel and Orry looked at each other. Neither of them had done anything to displease their father. And the light went off in Daniel's head. "Patrick? Patrick is the head of this little venture? Are you sure, Sir?"

"You notice Santori didn't fire at Emma? The one person the most dear to me. He didn't cause he had his orders, didn't he, Mac?"

"Could be, boss." He paused. "You accusing me, Don Andrea? You think it's me and not your son? You think because I saved your wife… it's me? She would never leave you for me… ever. Like she would never leave you for Patrick. And, boss, it's only the same as you knowing Janine still loves you. You have not touched her or done anything about it since your teens. And Jonas… she wanted a shot at you. You knew it, but you didn't go there. You didn't touch her. You have loyalty to your wife… just like I do to both you and Emma!"

"I do, Mac. But who found the camera in the bedroom, Mac? How did the brakes get cut on the Ferrari? Who saw Patrick kiss Emma? Who has something to gain from Andrea Pauli being his grandson?

Who, Mac?" and Vega got right up in Mac's face. "Who?" and Vega was yelling, his face turning red and his hand nearing his gun. "And whose son did I shoot and kill?" There it was! The point in question.

"It wasn't me, Mr. Vega. I have always been loyal to you. What does it take to prove to you that it's not me?" Mac protested very strongly. He was up against a very tough boss. Charlie and Alex were there, too. He was way outgunned. Even Mikey looked like he believed Vega.

"You have not always been loyal, Mac… you slept with my first wife… and you gave me cause not to believe you some years back. I think you remember that. I trusted you with my wife's life." Vega paused. "You want to prove yourself… go to the hospital. You know what to do!" and Vega turned away from Mac. He couldn't look him in the face. "Mikey… go with him." Vega opened the pool doors and stepped outside into the air. He was shaking. He hoped it was enough.

Emma stepped out behind him. He didn't turn around to face her. She leaned gently on his back and wrapped her arms around his waist. He folded his arms on hers and dipped his head. Emma thought that his tears touched her hands, and she cried on his back.

"Does Charlie know?" she asked quietly.

"Yes, and now you…"

"When did you know?"

"Last night for sure. I hoped I was wrong. Dear God, I hoped. I thought I was losing you, Emma. That's one of the reasons for the renewal of the vows."

"Oh God, Philip. I will never leave you. Ever. I love you so very very much. You have to know that."

"I do. The seeds were planted by others. Slowly… one at a time. Then the dreams… I believed you, but wasn't sure which one of them it was. But now I know. Charlie knew. I just didn't want to believe it, baby." Philip looked at her hand. There sat the ring. He knew she knew what the ring meant. To dishonor it was to die.

"Philip, can we go home soon? I mean really go home, maybe even Colorado. You, me and the children? You were so angry in there that I was worried for you. I don't want to lose you, Philip. I can't live without you. Please?"

"Christmas, baby. We will be there by then." He turned in her arms and looked down at her. Little Emma Sands, his one true love in life was there for him even now when she knew what was about to happen. He kissed her parted lips. She was the only one he trusted now and perhaps ever had. She had nothing to gain.

Vega wiped the tears from Emma's eyes and clung to her. How long they stood there, they didn't know, she dressed in a simple black dress most fitting for the occasion. And Vega all in black.

Vega heard the phone ring in the suite. Someone would answer it. He had left his cell there on purpose.

Charlie appeared at the door with Alex. Alex handed his boss the cell.

Philip let one hand go from Emma and put the cell to his ear. "Yeah…"

"It's done, boss. Finished," and Vega closed the cell and hurdled it into the pool.

"Andrea, give me your gun…"

And Vega handed it to Charlie Hill.

"Stay with him, Emma. Do not leave him alone for one second. Alex and I will be right here. You call if you need us," and Charlie gently closed the door.

Chapter 50

... the conclusion

Vega and Emma sat down on a lounger by the pool, and she curled up into his body. Philip could hear the talk in the room next to the pool. He tried to drown it out, but it wouldn't go away. All it had taken was a pillow over their head and a silencer on the end of a gun. And the job was done. One clean shot. There was no struggle, as he was held down. No one at the hospital would know till later when they found the body. Now it really was over. The Vega dynasty was safe.

Philip could hear Mikey's voice, loud and clear, and the other slightly muffled. He knew who it was... and Vega grieved.

Charlie was right. Emma dare not leave him on his own... not for a second.

Vega went over it once more in his mind. The flat tire, the cut brakes with the right timing, which threw any suspicion off the person driving it. The camera in the bedroom, watching what that man could never have. His arms round Emma, not once but twice... and he had saved her life, not letting Santori shoot her. For that Vega was glad.

"Philip... you want to go inside? Talk to them..."

He stopped her speaking. "Not yet... maybe later. You need something?"

"Some water..."

"Charlie," yelled Philip.

And Charlie appeared. "Don Andrea?"

"My wife would like some water and I would like scotch. Charlie…how did he die?" Philip felt Emma tense against him.

"He died well, Andrea. You would have been proud of him." And
Charlie went back inside to get their drinks.

"How does one die well? How the fuck does one die well?" and
Philip thumped the side of the lounger.

It shook Emma. "I don't know, Philip. I guess not as a coward
and traitor." It was all she could think of to say.

He looked at her in the fading light, and smiled a small smile for
her. She was braver than he was.

"The police will come. They will ask questions, they will go. Still
money talks in Vegas. Charlie made it talk. Tomorrow we will fly
home, take our children and the twins. I will teach Daniel all our
ways and, as soon as he is able, he will take my place. I have one place
to stop on the way to the airport."

The limos left the Villa at eight the next morning. They headed
for the airport, all except the one with Vega and Emma. Vinnie drove
them one last time and Alex rode shotgun. Vega had not slept at all
and Emma very little. His conscience weighed heavily and his face
betrayed his feelings. He hoped Father Murphy was there and would
see him. He couldn't blame him if he wanted no part of him, as Vega
felt he had desecrated God's house.

The limo pulled up by the long steps outside, blood stains still
smattered the concrete. Alex opened the door for his boss and Vega
turned to Emma, before he climbed out of the car.

"Emma, this is something I must do on my own. I beg your forgiveness and please wait here for me. The plane cannot leave with out
us and I will only be a short time. I have to say goodbye here. I cannot
take the memory home. It has to stay here."

Emma understood, even though her eyes filled with tears on his
behalf. She nodded her head to him.

Don Andrea climbed out of the car and walked slowly, but delib-
erately up the church steps. He reached the doors and pushed them
open wide. He could see the man in the first pew, sitting there staring

at the alter. Vega knew he would find him there. It's where he would have been if he had been ordered to shoot someone's son.

Vega moved up the pews to where the man sat alone, his blonde hair giving him away, and he stood waiting for the lone gun to see him.

The man looked up to Vega, his face wet with tears and lined from guilt. "Forgive me, Don Andrea. I could not do it. I could not kill your son, even though you killed mine. You were right; it's the hardest thing to do. I am not the man you are and never will be. Mikey did it. Always knew Mikey was tough. I came back with him last night, but I could not face you." As he spoke, Mac pulled the gun from the back of his jeans and handed it to his boss. "You have the right to use it, Don Andrea. I disobeyed you." And Mac Hunter wept openly in front of his Don.

Vega took the weapon from Mac's hand and aimed it at Mac's head. "I told you it was not easy to kill another's son. But Patrick is dead. I am told my son died well. He did not plead for his life. And now Emma and I go home with our family to carry on with our lives. Daniel will be the next Don. You, Mac," as Philip looked up at the statue of Mary and studied the stain glass window behind it, reflecting on the situation, "You should stay in Vegas awhile. Vinnie knows people you can stay with. When the time is right…" and Vega breathed a heavy sigh, heartfelt and sincere, "you should could home. We have a child to raise, you and I, a grandchild. And you are honor bound to love my wife as a daughter and protect her with your life. And I do believe you will."

Mac stared at his Don. He had showed compassion.

Philip Vega handed the gun back to Mac. "If you cannot do this…" and Vega said no more. He turned from Mac's pleading eyes. Vega crossed himself and walked back down the church and to the door, his solo footsteps echoing on the marble floor. He opened the big wooden doors.

The last thing Vega heard was a single gunshot. He didn't look back. Mac could do it after all.

Philip Vega walked outside into the morning sun. Now it was ended. He climbed into the waiting car and into his wife's arms and they sped off in the morning light to the plane and home. He reached for her hand and she clutched his fingers, and as Emma looked into his face, tears streamed down his cheeks. And Don Andrea's wife knew what had taken place.

■

www.ingramcontent.com/pod-product-compliance
Lightning Source LLC
Chambersburg PA
CBHW051824020726
47502CB00005B/1612

* 9 7 8 1 5 9 3 9 3 3 9 9 9 *